OTHER TITLES BY MONICA J. LINDER

what's in your hand

Shepley House

Monica J. Linder

The Twirl Press

Content warnings: Sexual abuse, neglect, murder, language

ISBN: 979-8-9928994-2-9

For Mom

Shepley House

Rumor Has It

her daughter drowned
in that pond.

Rumor has it
the body
was never found.

Rumor has it
she is still spotted
from time to time
drifting around the edge
in a flowing bloodstained gown.

Curled and Twisted

black iron gates
scarred by rust
screech open
to a pea gravel driveway
winding and crawling
up a secret spun path
guarded by treacherous trees
leading to the place called Shepley
a house long forgotten
a castle with grudges
a dwelling that frowns
and crumples its brows.

There will be no welcome
or mats rolled out
no greetings or shared smiles
and as I make my way
up the outstretched staircase
that's far from celebrating my arrival
I realize
there are long months ahead.

Shepley House, Rehabilitation Center

Biggest joke I've ever heard.
Rehabilitation, my ass.

If by rehabilitating
you mean head hunting
the crazies of the world
removing them from society
tossing them into a crumbling creepy castle
that's probably a rooming house
for ghosts and evil spirits
numbing them up with drugs
that make reality even more questionable
putting them to work scrubbing at filth
under the authority of "staff"
who look like they would benefit
from their own interventions
while hoping no one kills you in the meantime
then I guess you have yourself a deal.

Unfortunately for me
this isn't even my first visit to this place.

It is just my first time as the patient.

The Castle

is different than I remember.

It has been five years since I was last here
and somehow the ambiance of the place feels off.

When I was younger
I thought it was regal and beautiful.

I didn't understand why they called it
Shepley House

       not Shepley Castle
       or Shepley Palace.

Today, however, it feels like it fits.

Stone that once seemed unbreakable
is crumbling.

Gardens that were lush
       and pooling with color
             have faded to sepia
and gloom floats
       like a blanket
             suffocating hope and life.

The entry hall
         feels more like a vault
than a welcoming space.
         Although it is not dark
bone-colored stone
         makes me feel like I stepped
into a coffin
         and closed the lid.

A massive wrought iron chandelier
         dangles precariously
the chains holding it in place
         whisper jokes about viability.

A portrait of a young girl
         hangs on the wall to the left
of a sprawling staircase
         conviction in her eyes
something evocative, yet mysterious
         in her expression.

"Headmistress will be right with you,"
         a nurse says, as I stand here staring.

What a picture to have
         hanging in a place allegedly
designed to stabilize crazies.

As I stare at her face, so lifelike
        an eclipse of moths
float toward my line of vision.

I turn my head, startled
        and they almost seem
to change their tune
        to hurl themselves at me.

I cover my head with my arms and duck
        a myriad of wings flapping
as they pass
        and continue on
to wherever they were going.

"Emily Jones," someone hisses
        and I lower my arms.
I am guided to my room
        the haunting having already crossed me
and when the sound of shrieking
        rakes my ears
I hold a pillow over my head
        and left wondering
what has gone wrong
        to turn this once restorative home
to hell?

No wonder Annie never got better.

Ever Try Sharing A Parent

with the crazy sister?

The one who threatens to bash people's skulls in
when she's mad?

Who screams in restaurants
when her food doesn't taste
the way she wanted it to?

Who makes every moment miserable
because you never know when the next
explosion is coming?

All our money
Mama's love and attention wasted
trying to reason with someone
who threatens her life
while I watch.

"Poor Annie," they say.
"She's had it so hard."

Poor Annie?

No one thinks about Mama having to raise her

the meds
bills
interventions
therapists
hospital stays
broken windows
flat tires
cracked doors

steadily crushed hopes.

Or me watching

terrified.

Things Got A Little Easier

when Annie went to Shepley House.

The bills still flowed in
but at least our home was quiet
and Mama stopped crying herself
to sleep every night.

Finally
it was just me and Mama
and it was great.

We would visit Annie
on the weekends sometimes
though eventually that stopped.

Not that I minded.

I didn't particularly enjoy the drive
and it was hard
to look forward to seeing her
after everything she put Mama through.

But then Mama
started to date.

I should have been happy
for her.

She was alone for so long.

I should have wanted
that for her.

Jealous

Instead of being happy
that Mama was finally okay
I was jealous.

I waited for it to be just me and Mama
and now she wanted to date.

They weren't awful, her boyfriends
objectively speaking.

There was Mitch
with the baseball caps and peanuts.
He tossed me a bag and said:
"Eat up, kid."

I poured Miralax in his soup
and after a long
(and messy, I'm guessing)
stint in the bathroom
he walked quickly out of the house
saying a glanceless goodbye to Mama
never to return.

Then there was Joey.

So tall
and so quiet.

I stashed a toad
in the front seat of his car
and he hollered
louder than a fog horn at dawn
when it hopped out at him
ribbet, ribbeting away.

Mama knew it was me that time.
She actually laughed
about how high pitched his shriek was.

But she scolded me
asked what I needed.
I needed her.
No boyfriend, no Annie.
Just her.
Her and me.
Me and her.

She still dated after that
but she stopped bringing them home
and that was fine by me.

Except now, it was lonely.

A Boy At School

showed me where to hide
and do "grown up things."

He hid with me
and I learned.

Cried
but never there.

Just laid and waited.

If I wanted it to be over faster
all I had to do was make a sound
or move like I liked it.

But either way
it never took long.

Sophomore Year

I met Pierce.

He turned paper to flowers
tucking a bouquet
in my backpack one day.

We started hanging out
after school.

He'd come over
and I didn't have to worry
because Mama was rarely home.

We read books together
threw orange peels at at each other
and one day
he kissed me.

That Day I Knew

why songs are written about

magic

why dreamers use the word

perfect

how this simple touch turns a frog to a

prince

Pierce's lips on

mine

lends definition to

divine

side to side
giving and taking
sprinting and crawling
every piece of me

awakening

with
Pierce
and

me

kissing.

Two Years

countless smiles
and a promised future.

Pierce.
Me.
The world.
Kids.
A home.
And love.
So much love.

All the things a girl dreams of.

The things I grew up outside of
because my childhood was marked
by abandonment, an unstable sibling
and loneliness.

Wiped away by a boy
who cares for me.

Remembering

"I know you from somewhere," a boy with curly hair, twinkling eyes, and shiny brown muscles says, disrupting my silent life review, making me suddenly aware of the bucket in my hands. I've been assigned kitchen duty for today which means, amongst other things, an endless amount of scrubbing. The boy looks familiar but I can't figure out if I actually know him.

"Wait..." he says. "Annie?"

He knows my sister.

"No," I say. "I'm Emily. Annie's my sister."

"Oh." He stops, brow furrowed. "I don't remember Annie having a sister. That's weird."

Not to me. Annie took up enough space for both of us.

"Yeah," I say. "I always ran around the grounds when we visited, playing hide-and-seek and throwing pebbles in the pond." I stare at him for a second longer. "I remember you! You're Kit. You spilled pink lemonade on my dress. You live...next door, right?"

"Yep," he says. "I'm just hired help these days." He flings the curtain covering the space beneath the commercial kitchen sink open to pull out a giant tin bucket. "Damn, you look so much like Annie. She made the most beautiful paintings." He pauses. "So what did you do to land yourself here?" Kit asks, waiting for the bucket to fill.

"It doesn't matter," I say, climbing on the countertop, tiptoeing to reach the tops of the cabinets.

"Oh, come on," he says. "You're no fun."

Maybe he'll stop asking if I just tell him. "I tried to run away with my boyfriend," I say, my shoulder aching from the reach.

Kit busts out laughing and I instantly wish I would have kept it to myself.

"Not that it's any of your business," I remind him.

"Tried to run away, huh?" Kit says. "How adorable. So where's your knight in shining armor now then?"

With one last flick of my wrist, I hop down, brush the cloud off my apron. "Not in this hellhole," I say. "Which gives him one up on you now, doesn't it?"

The House

These staircase steps groan louder than a cow giving birth. Even if we were allowed to snoop, it wouldn't matter, because every step anyone takes reverberates throughout the rest of the house. There is nothing quiet or polished about these ruins. Every inch I've been through so far creaks, moans, screams, or makes some sort of unpleasant sound, while also being clouded by dust, and something I can't quite figure out.

With the amount of cleaning we do all day, you would think the place would be spotless, but surfaces are still caked with grit, making me feel like I'm constantly in need of a shower.

And that's not even mentioning the people.

Headmistress Harrison is what they call her, but a more fitting description would be Sergeant or Tyrant. Tall and bent crooked like a fetch stick, stark white skin with wrinkles like meringue that is only visible on her face and hands because every other part of her is covered in crisp black garb, pulled tight at the waist of her dress with a nondescript belt and a beguiling emerald brooch that lays flat against her pale throat.

I don't dare make eye contact because I'm certain she would find that to be "insolence" or "impertinence." These are words I hear today as I shampoo the rug that leads to her office.

Apparently some girl was caught stealing food from the kitchen. Toilet duty for a month.

Tilly says toilet duty isn't that bad.

Short and scrawny, uncooked spaghetti noodles for hair, teeth that would benefit from brushing, and eyes that make me want to stay on her good side, Tilly seems like the kind of girl who wouldn't squawk at anything, no matter how disgusting or undesirable it was.   "The boys is nasty, but even cleanin' up after them ain't the worst duty t'have."

"So if not that, then what?" I ask.

She shudders. "Easy. Takin' care of Laurel."

According to Tilly

Laurel is the craziest of them all. So crazy you have to do something pretty heinous to get on Laurel duty. Who knows if she'll attack you or hug you? "Ya won't know until she does one fing or th' othuh."

Tilly lowers her voice to the slightest whisper and leans her face against the broomstick in her hands. "Let's just say people have—" she mouths the word *died* "—'n there."

"Have you ever been on Laurel duty?"

Tilly grimaces. "Yeah, once." "She didn't hate me though. I thought I was gonna chit myself I was so scared of goin' in there. 'N I figured well if I'm already dyin' I might as well go out kickin'. 'N so I snatched 'er a choc'late morsel from the kitch'n. 'N let's just say she didn't attack me, but she told me fings. She is..." Tilly motions a swirly with her finger next to her ear and whistles. "Don't recommend."

The Rules

Always	do your chores
No	exploring or going anywhere
	you weren't specifically directed to
Do	what you are told
Be	respectful
Take	your meds
Don't	ask questions
Keep	your head down
Mind	your own business
	and never, under any circumstances
Go	in Headmistress's office.

The Unspoken Rules

AKA the stuff that can really get you in trouble
according to Tilly.

Appear   busy at all times
Stay   away from the common areas
                unless you are cleaning
Don't   be noticed, for anything, good or bad
Avoid   Headmistress at all costs

"Basically," I summarize—
"Don't exist unless as a housecleaner
or mind-numbed robot."

"Couldn't 'a said it better
m'self," Tilly says.

And if there's one thing I learned
from growing up with Annie
it's that the pills they call "meds"
don't actually improve anything.

Every single drug they give me is getting flushed.

Hints

Don't be doin' anyfin' stupid when Feller's around either," Tilly warns. "She's worser 'n Headmistress."

Ms. Feller is Headmistress Harrison's servant, sidekick, accomplice, whatever you want to call her, and she's as creepy as the Headmistress, if in a different way.

Short and round, like all it would take is a push and she'd go rolling, not quite unkempt, but certainly not well-maintained like Headmistress, and a notable feature of striking eyes that send a shiver down my spine, I quickly note that I'll be doing everything I can to avoid eye contact with her moving forward.

Tilly says Ms. Feller used to be a patient here before she became staff. Tilly also says she's not to be trusted, and she makes a good point. "Can't trust an'one who'd choose t' stay at Shepley. Lucky for ya, or maybe not dependin' on how ya fink, ya got here just 'n time to get ready fer th' annual ball."

"Annual ball?" I ask. "Why would a place like this have a ball?"

"Fundraiser," Tilly says. "Or like I like t' call 'em fun-scrapers."

"Ew," I say.

"Yer tellin' me. I got here just 'n time for it last year, and it sucked. We gotta make the place look all—"she motions with saint-like expression—"fancy, like an'one gives a chit. So all these rich old farts can come hear 'bout fixin' us 'n our 'issues' 'n flap their greens in the Headmistress's d'rection, like they're part of some great cause." Tilly practically spits the words out.

"Do we get to go?" I ask. Sounds horrid all around, but being able to partake in the festivities would make it a mite more tolerable.

She wrinkles her nose. "Where do ya think ya are? Disneyland?"

"Doesn't matter anyway," I say, ignoring the jab. "I'm gonna be gone by then."

Out of here.

Back to reality.

Back to Pierce.

Pierce

Beautiful
Smart
Creative

the one   I was supposed to
                 run away with
Pierce

                 the one I was
                 going to be with
Pierce

                 the one I want to
                 spend my life with
At night

                 his eyes are
all
I   see
remember

                 the way he looked at me
Pierce

                 the one
                 who didn't show

Pierce   the one who
                 landed me
                 here.

Daydreaming

"Why is your head always in the clouds?" Kit asks. "You won't get out of here if you keep acting like that. They'll think you're actually crazy."

"Why are you in here anyway?" I say, ignoring the rest. "I thought you only did outside duties?"

But he ignores my question. "I know that look. You've got a special someone on your mind." His voice is taunting and I'm annoyed.

"Don't you have something to do?" I say.

"Yeah," he says. "And I'm doing it. It's you I was concerned about."

I look down to find water dripping from my rag all over the floor in a puddle.

"Damn it, Kit. Why didn't you say something sooner?"

"I was wondering how long it would take you to notice. So what's his name?"

"None. Of. Your. Business," I say, desperate for a subject change. "What's the fastest way out of here?"

"Not bathing the floor," he chuckles.

I glare and he says: "You know, showing some great insight into what got you here and a plan as to how you're not going to do it again. Some sign of stability."

"Thanks," I say. "Real helpful. Basically act like I committed a crime."

He shrugs. "Yeah. Pretty much. From what I've seen, works every time."

Cleaning Duties

Gardening. Weeding. Dusting. Mopping. Scrubbing. They all conjure up the same feelings. Make something lovely, while I absorb dirt and ugly, crawl into bed sore, marked up, and exhausted.

I haven't figured out what the gig I want is. One away from eyes and away from the rest of the household. But it seems like everywhere I go, there's a presence. I don't even know what a presence is, other than to say sometimes when I am alone, I feel there is something else, someone else in the room watching me.

I find myself turning quickly, moving my shoulders, flicking at air, because it sure feels like something or someone is lingering. But no matter how I move, I come up with empty palms and spider sensations running up and down my spine.

If I stop what I'm doing and sit really still, I hear whispering and one simple phrase that seems to float around and around, like a merry go round. *Set me free.*

Even garden duty gives me the heebie jeebies. Along the box hedges and rose bushes that circle the space are winged stone angels and nothing about them seems like decor.

They look

like real people.

One girl, with her hand to her face, another bent down her face in her arms, like she's sobbing.

Another, a woman, high cheekbones, resolute thin lips, one hand at her side, one up, mid air, like she was right in the middle of saying something.

Still another, a couple in an embrace, clinging to each other as if their lives depended on it, the woman's face turned away, sadness clouding her eyes. He stares at her cheek, chasing another moment, grasping at something slipping through his fingers.

A common thread seems to hold them all together in a frozen moment no one asked for. And even though I know it's not possible, they all seem to whisper the same phrase. *I am not free.*

I also can't quite put my finger on why something major still feels undone with the amount of hours that go into caring for it all.

Ronnie is hired help, responsible for overseeing ground maintenance by directing the work of the residents, while also putting in his own work. Yet the work of the other residents is invisible somehow and it seems like no matter how hard I work alongside Ronnie, it feels unkept.

"Say there, Miss Emily," Ronnie says, adjusting his baseball cap and tucking his hair around his ears. "You're really good at this stuff here. Mind giving me a hand?"

He motions to little saplings springing up around the trees. "We gotta take care of those. I'm gonna get started on the mowing."

I like having a defined task, so I get to work circling the trees that line the driveway, ripping out the saplings, weeds, and anything else that's growing around them that's not supposed to be there.

The buzz of the mower becomes a comforting drone after a while and I realize that in a weird way, the sound is comforting. Maybe it somehow feels more domestic than the rest of what I spend my time doing here.

Ah, that's it. It feels like home. A familiar sound and smell to making my way home from school or going for a walk with Pierce. As silly as it is, I revel in the momentary solace, grateful for familiarity.

Time slips by and then the buzz stops. I am nearly at the end of the driveway at this point, having worked my way down the winding path, and Ronnie has mowed the grass just about right up to where I am.

"Hot out here," he says, pulling a hanky out of the pocket on his overalls and wiping his forehead.

"How long have you been here?" I ask.

"Oh, you know, few hours or whatever it's been."

"No, I mean, like how long have you worked here in your life?"

"Durn," Ronnie says. "I dunno. Feels like forever." Ronnie has one eye that goes off to the side when you're talking to him so I can't tell where he's actually looking, which is only slightly unsettling. "Probably twenty years."

"Does the place seem different to you now, as opposed to how it used to?" I ask. He, of anyone, ought to see the subtle changes. Maybe he could help me identify what feels off.

"Can't think of what you mean," Ronnie says. "I'm just here to mow and look after the grounds, see. What you mean, different?"

"Never mind," I say.

"Well seein' as how you're here to work," Ronnie says, "Better get back to work."

"Right," I say.

The First Time

It's the worst in the garden in mid afternoon. Between
sweltering heat, lack of shade, and so many bugs and critters,
I am dripping and crawling, after a few minutes of work.

Today I distract myself by pretending to clean the
statues, even though they are stone and don't really need
cleaning. But it gives me a chance to stop and stare, take
them in, and each time I do, I end up wondering if it's heat
or my eyes playing tricks on me.

I am picking weeds cropping out of the rose bush
next to the angel with the high cheekbones, but find myself
more distracted with taking her in. The bodice of her dress
is form fitted, a V neckline accentuating her defined
collarbone, long, slender neck, beautiful face, hair gathered
up loosely, curls surrounding her cheeks and running down
her back.

I run my finger along the lines on her hand,
pushing dirt particles out of the cracks between her fingers,
stare at her face. There is something about the posture of
her lips that suggests she is not an easy person to get along
with. She was halted with a word or two on her lips. Likely
choice ones. I run my hand along the skirt of her dress to

the bottom where a small pile of dirt is gathering in the hem. Kneeling down, I hold the handful of weeds in one hand and scoop dirt out with the other, which leaves me in a precarious position.

A sudden wind rushes me, shoving me off balance and ripping the stems from my hand. I fall into the bush beside the statue, thorns stabbing my face and shoulders. The stems circle my head in a green cyclone.

What a strong gust.

Except there is no wind in Louisiana in summer, and certainly not in the swamps of the Thibodeaux Basin.

As I regain my balance, picking the thorns and brush out of my hair, I glance up at the statue's face, and I could swear her mouth turns up ever so slightly at the corner into a smirk.

Making Sense of It

It's just the heat getting to me, I tell myself over and over. *The heat and this place.* I got sent here for high risk behavior, not psychosis. I'm not seeing what I'm seeing. My mind is just stressed and desperate to fill in some blanks.

But today as I scrape moss forming on the feet of the girl with her face in her arms, I could swear I feel the rock moving, hear a cry escaping her.

Suddenly feeling faint, I grab the stone ankle poking out from the hem of the carved dress, attempting to steady myself, wipe sweat off my forehead with my shirt.

I have to figure out how to get assigned something else to do around here. Something that doesn't make me question my own sanity.

Then Again

Can't guarantee
I am not crazy.

Maybe
I'm the one

who needs to be set free.

But Then It Happens Again

And this time, it's even more frightening.

I am trying to find the end or beginning of a vine, crawling its way up the angel couple, but instead, I lose myself in their expressions.

The way he holds her so tenderly. One hand is tucked under her wing supporting her waist, as if he was in the middle of dipping her in a dance, the other hand caresses the side of her neck.

But her face is turned outward, away from him, away from the intimacy, and the grief I noted the first time I saw them strikes me the same today. Maybe even more so.

The vine follows the curve of her body dripping down her breast, following along to the hem of her dress. I slip my fingers under the green rope, but the vine coils around my hand and thorn-like razor blades break my skin.

I recoil from the pain yanking my hand back, but the vine crawls up my wrist, twists its way around my arm, and rakes lines, blood dripping on the angel's dress.

I scream for help, and with every bit of force I can find, rip myself away, causing me to lose my balance, and fall backward. I flick the tears of my eyes with the not bloody hand and wrap the bloody hand in my shirt.

I know

how this is going to look.

I know

what they're going to say.

"You alright there, Em?" Damn it. Of course Kit would be the one to find me.

"What does it look like?" I say, pretending I'm just hot and annoyed, not hurt.

"What happened?" he asks, and then when he sees the blood on the statue says: "Didn't anyone warn you about Devil's Hair? You can't be touching that. It's poisonous."

"Do you think I would have done it if I had known that?" I ask.

He extends his hand, but I pull myself up without using it, not mentioning that poison is the least of my worries.

Thankfully

The staff don't think there was any intention behind my injury, and no incident report is written. The nurse wraps my hand up, gives me an extra pill for the pain, which for once I'm tempted to take, tells me to rest in my room for the rest of the day.

But all being locked up in my room does is start the hamster wheel in my head rolling. I'm not supposed to be here. I'm stuck in this house for crazies, instead of laying on a beach with Pierce. It wasn't supposed to be this way.

Now I have to sit here, wondering if I'm losing my mind, or if these things that keep happening have some sort of basis in reality.

So maybe I don't know enough about toxic plants in Louisiana or about hallucinations from heat and whatever it is that happens to cause a breeze when that's not actually possible.

There are explanations for (almost) everything I have encountered so far. There must be. I'm not going crazy. It is just this place.

And the more important question is, how am I going to get out of here?

If Stone Could Move

If stone could move

        a castle

        wouldn't seem permanent.

If stone could move

        home

        could be transported.

Seasons of life

        would flow from one to another

           Anguish would diminish

              leaving joy to be discovered.

      Maybe my life

             wouldn't feel like a lie

      Maybe I'd remember

             existing before goodbye

But stone does not move

        and there is no revolution

so I remain numb

        crouched in my own delusion.

Rumors

I'm weeding between the cracks in the cement surrounding a wishing pool, the same wishing pool I threw rocks in when I was little, visiting Annie here.

It is so different from what I remember. As a little girl, I thought it was big enough to drown in. Now I see it is not any bigger than any other fountain body and certainly not big enough to drown in.

My memory of where it was placed is also distorted, so close to the edge of the property line, pristine and manicured next to Kit's family property, which contrasts as wild and overgrown.

Kit seems to have found the only cleared out bit of shade on their side of the property to clean an old grey station wagon in.

"Is this place haunted?" I ask him.

He stops, tosses a ratty buff into the plastic red bucket next to the tire, wipes his brow and blinks. "What do you think, Em? No one's asked me that in years."

"I don't know," I say. "I know it sounds stupid."

Kit bends down, pulls the sopping rag out of the bucket, wrings it, turns back to the car and starts scrubbing again. "Well, what would a castle like Shepley be without a ghost or two?"

As soon as he says it, I feel ridiculous.

"Maybe you're the one who belongs here," I say, and he laughs.

"You've heard about Marguerite, right?" he asks, and I'm all ears.

Marguerite

The Headmistress's only daughter. It's her portrait that rests in the entry hall.

According to Kit, Marguerite was the inspiration for Headmistress opening Shepley House to begin with. Headmistress wanted a different life for her daughter who suffered challenges that the rest of the world didn't seem to have space for.

Kit says she disappeared a few years ago and no one ever figured out where she went. It was rumored that she killed herself, but her body was never recovered, and although she was "a little loony", she seemed like she was on the mend when it happened.

"Headmistress was a wreck as any parent would be. Beside herself with grief." Kit sighs. "I don't think she's ever really gotten over it."

"Well, how could she?" I ask. "To just wonder and never have an answer would be enough to drive anyone bonkers." I trail off, wondering if Mama felt the same way when Annie stopped contacting us. Never really thought about that before.

"Damn," I say. "Her only daughter."

"Exactly," Kit says. "So I guess you could say there's definitely space for a spirit or two to linger here."

Laying the rag on the side of the bucket, he walks into the bright sunshine and plops down on the edge of the fountain. "Matter of fact, you've heard the rumors about this, right? How sometimes Marguerite is spotted here? Supposedly it's the last place she was seen alive that night."

I find myself inching away from the fountain's edge, walking instead toward the garden and Kit follows.

"Know anything about the statues?" I ask. "Like who made them or where they came from?"

Kit throws his hands up. "Your guess is as good as mine. It seems the collection has slowly grown over the years. I bet they're purchased with proceeds from the annual gala."

"They speak," I say, as we approach the statue of the couple, and then when Kit looks at me, I explain: "You know, artistry and all that."

"Isn't that the job of a good artist, to give an interpretation that feels so real, that the lines between reality and art are blurred?"

"What kind of high-falutin' mumbo jumbo was that?" I snort. "Mr. Country Boy trying to be all critical thinking."

Kit shrugs. "You ain't the only one with multiple layers, Emily."

"But, these," I say, redirecting the conversation back. "They give me the same feeling this whole place gives me." Even as the words fall from my mouth, I can tell he sees past what I'm saying.

"You think they're haunted?"

I pretend to think for a moment. "Haunted? No. Alive? Perhaps."

He scoffs, but waits for me to go on.

"Have you ever looked at their faces? There is nothing generic about them. Just look at the way this one mourns. What happened to her?"

Kit laughs, and I know it's coming. "At the rate you're going," he says. "If you weren't nuts when you got here, you will be, by the time you leave. If you leave."

And just the way he says it makes me wonder if people frequently don't leave.

Noticed

As if being in a constant state of creeped out and questioning reality wasn't enough, despite my best efforts to not be noticed, I can't seem to stay out of the eye of Headmistress Harrison.

Every time she passes, I trip over my own feet, bump into something, or find some way to draw attention to myself. Attention I don't want.

Today I'm cleaning the walls in the entry hall, which requires a lot of up and down on the ladder because of how high the ceilings are.

I'm doing just fine, but of course the moment Headmistress walks through the room, I trip and fall, pulling the ladder down with my ankle. The ladder crashes to the floor, making an awful clattering sound, and I am sure I must have broken something. I grab onto the banister in an attempt to catch myself, and the pressure on my injured hand causes it to bleed again, blood pooling under the bandage.

The Headmistress's neck snaps in my direction, her eyes climbing the staircase. "What are you doing, you clumsy rat?" she breathes, making me wish she would just scream at me, because this is far more terrifying.

Then she squints at me. "Who is... Come here, child."

I want to inform her that I am only technically a child for a few more weeks, but the words catch in my throat. Tiptoeing down the staircase toward her, I cradle my injured hand, hoping the bleeding will subside soon.

"Ah," Headmistress says when she sees my face. "Jones. Emily Jones. Sister of the illustrious Annie Jones. How could I forget?"

She stares me down disdainfully, and when her eyes return to my face, she says: "Don't let me catch you dawdling again. And clean this mess up. Make yourself useful for once."

Circumvention

What do I do to earn phone privileges?"
I ask Tilly.
"Like how long do I have to follow the rules
before I can level up and make a call?"

Tilly snorts. "You ain't gonna get calls here.
Fastest way out is out."

I don't ask what the consequences are
for breaking a rule
but how bad could it be?

I'm already here.

Trade Offs & Payoffs

Breaking some rules ------------> Getting to talk to Pierce

Might get assigned ------------> Talk to the only person
to a crazy person   I'm crazy about

Might die ------------> At least I'll be happy

Sometimes
you gotta swing

      big risks

            for

                big payoffs.

Acquiring Help

"Hey, mind if I run in your house and borrow the phone, so I can make a quick call?" I ask.

"Now what kind of friend would I be if I let you do that?" Kit asks, raising an eyebrow.

"A good one," I say. "Sharing is caring."

Kit shakes his head. "I've heard the stories. Trust me—you don't want to chance it."

I feel a pout coming on. "Who's gonna see me? Who's gonna tell?" I know I sound desperate, but I might as well beg. What other options do I have?

"Not happening. Find some other sucker."

Failed

If I can't use Kit's, I'm screwed.

I can't send a letter.

Even if I could find
       a stamp
       and envelope
       and paper

and managed to sneak to the mailman
without getting caught
Pierce would have no way
of contacting me back.

There's gotta be a phone here somewhere.

There has to be and I will find it.

I have to.
My sanity depends on it.

Rights

Tilly insists it'll be ages before I leave, and I might as well get comfortable, but that's the furthest thing from my mind. "Settle in, or the eyes 'n ears of this place will do it f'r ya."

"When you talk like that, I feel like we are in prison," I say.

"Ain't we?" Tilly says. "I mean, what freedoms d'ya have? And when was th' last time ya talked to yer fam'ly? See what I mean?"

Her question jolts me.

Mama. I have been here for close to three weeks now, and have been so focused on surviving daily life and on figuring out a way to contact Pierce, I hadn't even thought about Mama. "Is it legal for them to do this? Keep us locked up here, without even a word from the outside?"

"Legal?" Tilly laughs. "We're crazy, 'member? We ain't got rights."

Mama

Mama's plan was to spend the summer in Europe with her boyfriend. I hadn't minded, because Pierce and I were supposed to start our happily ever after. After everything went down and she brought me here, she didn't tell me if her plan had changed or if she was still going to go.

I hate that she brought me here, and I hope her plans for her own summer were disrupted. After so many years focused on Annie and then on herself, she decided to get involved in my life when I finally had a plan of my own. It might have worked out if she had just let things be.

My Plan Was Simple

Walk   the stage
Kiss   Mama's proud face
               and then once everyone started
               getting drunk at the after party
Sneak off   to Pierce's car
               already packed
               with a few things
               and drive.

Two stops
and that would get us to Michigan
where we'd start our new life together.

I'd send Mama a card once we got there
let her know I was safe
and we'd be good.

A simple plan that went to shit
and I missed all the signs.

That Morning

Graduation morning
      I texted Pierce:

Today's our day, baby!

Should have been my first clue
when he didn't respond.

Pierce
      always
            responds.

I figured he was busy
      packing or something.

I was mostly ready
but I combed through the house
tossing snacks for the road in a bag
grabbing a pot and a few utensils
Mama wouldn't miss.

At noon
I changed into the simple white lace dress
I bought for graduation and did my makeup
simple, classic red lips.

When the doorbell rang
I ran to the door
and there he was.

Perfect.
Beautiful.
My forever.

He picked me up
spun me around
and kissed me.

"I missed you," I said.

"Last time you'll have to," he said
tossing a wink

        with those eyes.

"Mama's gonna meet us there,"
I said, taking his hand
and walking toward my bedroom.

You Messed My Hair Up

I said.

"I messed your hair up,"
he acknowledged.

Pierce Helped Me

load my suitcase
and the few other things I collected
into his car.

I couldn't wait
for the ceremony and party
to be over with
so we could get on the road.

When we got in the car
to drive to graduation
he said: "There's something
I need to tell you, Emmy."

"We got five hours of driving
tonight, baby," I said.

Plenty of time was what I thought.

"I need you to know..." he said.

And I turned the radio up
made the speakers crackle
told him he was ruining the mood.

"Hold me closer
tinyy daaaaancer," I belted
and Pierce smiled
but not like he usually does
when I sing.

So I sang louder of course.

Another Possibility

The next time I'm on hallway duty, I stay as close to the door as I can while I clean, hoping to catch a glimpse of the inside of Headmistress's office. If there is one part of this place that couldn't run without a phone, it would be her work. Right? But I don't end up needing to catch a glimpse because I overhear a one-sided conversation with a tell-tale click at the end. Magnificent.

"Who cleans Headmistress's office," I ask Tilly, when I bump into her in the hallway.

Tilly's eyes bulb at my question and she shakes her head. "No one goes in her office. No one. 'member the rules?"

"Yeah, but not even Ms. Feller?" I prod.

"Nope."

"Not even to clean?" I ask.

She shakes her head again, eyes still crazy round.

"What are you not telling me, Tilly?" I press.

"Nothin'," she says. "Rumors is all."

And for once, much to my chagrin, Tilly's lips are as sealed as she claims.

I really don't want to invite more attention from whatever it is that lingers around this place, but I have to talk to Pierce. That would give me enough strength to power through until my birthday, when I can get the hell out of here.

Only problem is, I don't think I've ever seen Headmistress Harrison leave Shepley, so if I can't be assigned to clean in there, figuring out another way in might be an issue.

Exploring

"Does the Headmistress ever leave this place?" I ask Kit.

"Ha," he says, not a laugh. "No."

Ugh. More sneaking will have to be done.

If there's never going to be a good time, I'm just doing educated guessing, and worst case, I end up getting assigned to Laurel duty.

Hope I don't die.

In Retrospect

I probably could have gotten out of there without getting caught, had I not spotted something that disrupted every bit of concentration I had.

Something

      I

         would

            recognize

               anywhere.

                       Something

                   that

            in no way

         shape

      or form

belonged there.

Was It Worth It?

Pros:

- I made it into her office.
- I located the phone.
- I managed to dial Pierce.

Cons:

- He didn't pick up.
- I heard footsteps while I was still in there.
- I thought they passed.
- They did not.
- I have a million more questions than I did before.

No More Luck

I thought I could convince Feller to keep it between us by swearing it was a mistake and I was just lost.

Unfortunately, I have no such luck. Straight to solitary, and then Laurel duty.

The Worst Part About Solitary

is how loud your own thoughts get.

Why didn't Pierce answer?
Probably didn't recognize the number.

                                    Or maybe
                                    he was busy.

            Busy with what?
                        I wouldn't know.

                                    How is he?

                        Is he okay?

Does he miss me?

                        God, I miss him
                                    so damn much.

When am I going to get out
of this place?

                        Am I losing my mind being here?

It feels like I am
but maybe that's just because
I'm in solitary.

How is Mama doing?

Did she go to Europe?

Did she take her hard earned trip?

I hope she's not worrying
too much about me.

I'll be fine
if I can figure out
how to get out of here.

The Necklace

And then
as I retrieve
what I stumbled on
in Headmistress's office
from the pile of hair on my head
where I had tucked it
turn it over in my hand
all the rest of my thoughts
are pushed to the side.

Dainty gold chain
  with tiny cut emeralds
forming a flower completed by
  an almost not visible it's so small
sparkly diamond in the middle
  forming the belly of the bloom
her initials, A.J.
  engraved on the back.

Emeralds
  Annie's and my birthstone
and because our birthdays
  are so close together
we often celebrated them
  at the same time.

I remember the year
        Mama gave her this.

Mama used to give us
        a couple little gifts
like chapstick or gum
        and one big gift.

My big gift that year
        was a jute bracelet
with little wooden beads
        twisted through it.
I remember looking up
        after Mama finished helping me
tie it onto my wrist
        to see Annie's face light up
like Mama had just put her
        in charge of the stars
and while she squealed, hugging Mama
        I was seething
with jealousy.

But of course
        I couldn't show
my disappointment
        because I was Emily
Mama's good girl.

Annie was the difficult one
        and I did what I was supposed to.
After all, what would Mama do
        if she had two Annies?
Probably end up
        in some sort of facility herself.

No, it was my job
        to hold it together
to be consistent, reliable,
        and well-behaved.

So I smiled at Annie
        said: "How lovely"
instead of throwing an Annie sized hissy fit
        ripping the necklace from her
and keeping it for myself.

Annie didn't have anything else
        she clung to
like that necklace.

It seemed to become a source of pride for her
        but also a source of comfort.

On good days, she sported it proudly
        flicking her hair behind her shoulders
to make sure it was visible.

On bad days, squeezing it in her fist
        while curled up in the fetal position
screaming.

I never had a chance to let my feelings subside
        because she refused to take it off
and it hung right at the top of her neck
        so it was always visible.

A constant reminder
        that our whole life revolved around her
that she was the reason we couldn't
        afford to do anything nice or fun
no random trips to the ice cream store
        because every bit of Mama
went to stabilizing Annie
        and sometimes, often
not even that was enough.

So this necklace
        that I hated so much
but that meant the world to my sister
        would never
have parted ways with her
        without some significant
circumstances.

And how it came to land
        piled up and dusty
behind the phone receiver
        is certainly
beyond me

but one thing I know for sure is
        Annie would never
have left this necklace behind
        without a fight.

Laurel

When I finally get out of solitary, I have two weeks of Laurel duty. I don't dare attempt a sneak to the kitchen. Not for this. Better just hope that the self defense I learned from growing up with Annie serves me now.

Laurel's dark skin and dark hair contrast her all-white uniform almost comically. None of the rest of us wear uniforms so this is the first I've seen. When she spots me, her face scrunches up like she recognizes me but doesn't quite believe what her eyes are telling her. "Annie?"

"I'm Emily," I say. "Annie is my sister."

The connection seems to thrill her because she jumps up, and before I have a chance to move away, she throws her arms around me. Remembering what Tilly said, I am about to yank myself away from Laurel when she sighs: "Annie was my best friend here. I miss her."

She lets me go, and I exhale a long breath of relief, slipping a hand into my pocket, to touch the necklace. "How long has it been since you've seen her?" I ask.

Laurel sighs. "I don't have the firmest grip on time. You'd have to ask someone else." Somehow I feel I'll need to ask Laurel so much more but I'll let her lead for a bit.

Still squinting, she asks: "So what'd you do to get in charge of me?"

"Snuck into Headmistress Harrison's office."

Her eyes widen and she raises a hand. Still slightly on edge and unsure, I put my arms up but she laughs. A belly laugh. A genuine laugh. An outside world laugh. "Trying to high five you, silly," she says. "That took some ovaries. You have spice like your sister. I like it."

Not the response I was expecting, but somehow it makes me like her more. "Thanks," I say, lowering my arms slowly, still somewhat on edge, waiting for her to flip.

"What happened to your hand?" she asks, motioning to the lines, still a little raw.

"Some stupid vine in the garden attacked me," I explain. "Devil's Hair I think it's called?"

Laurel's nose scrunches up again, like I'm making something up, but she doesn't ask and changes the subject again. "So what'd you want in the office?" she asks. "See anything creepy?"

I'm not sure what kind of a question "see anything creepy?" is, and I can't help but wonder why she would ask.

"I just wanted to use the phone," I say, instantly regretting telling her that. I don't know her well enough yet to be sharing anything like that. "And no, I didn't see anything."

Just the necklace I stole that belongs to my sister, so technically it's not stealing.

Nosy

"You've been awfully invisible lately," Kit says when he sees me next.

"Bending rules has a way of doing that to you," I say, and he smirks.

"You don't even look sorry," he notes gleefully.

"Well I'm not exactly," I explain. "I had a need and I did my best to take care of it."

"And how did that work out for you?" he asks.

"Well," I say. "I guess it depends on how you look at things."

"And how do you look at things?" he presses.

I shrug. "Seeing as how you aren't exactly on my side, I don't think I need to be telling you how I'm looking at things, now do I? Well anyway, I better be going. I have a patient to see after now.

Reckoning

Laurel doesn't strike me as dangerous at all. In fact, the more time I spend around her, I don't see any signs that she is missing a few screws, other than the scars on her neck, and how she bites herself sometimes while we are talking. But the things she says make sense. I wonder if she flushes her drugs too.

As soon as the nurse leaves, Laurel flips a switch. So when she starts to say things like "it's not actually safe here" and "you should be careful", I want to know so much more.

"I mean, we've all heard the rumors," I say, baiting her. "I just don't think all they are is rumors." I want her to tell me what she knows, about the statues in the garden, about the things I keep hearing, and now about the necklace in my pocket, but I can't, not yet. Just to be on the safe side.

The most important thing is for me to get out of here, back to Pierce, and not even my curiosity get in the way of that. But she has a totally different story to tell me than what I was expecting.

Theories

Laurel's explanation, that apparently she and my sister pieced together, is that Marguerite didn't kill herself but was murdered here on the grounds. No one knows why or by who, but it happened the night she disappeared, the night of the annual ball.

Laurel says the only thing they could think of was that it was someone here who did it, and not another patient but someone "with all their crayons, y'know. You see, your sister and I spent a lot of time on this."

So many questions form, as she gives her explanation, and despite my resolve moments prior, I am unable to stop them from spilling out. "But how many people could that possibly be and who would have motivation to do so? Why do you think it was a staff or guest and not another patient?"

Laurel sighs. "I think Annie had it figured out. I think it's part of why she left the way she did. We went through everyone who was there that night, everyone who knew Marguerite. No one, I mean, no one was the killing type. You'd have to really be a killer to want someone like

Marguerite dead. The staff on the other hand... Have you seen some of them? I'm honestly safer in here." She motioned to the walls of her room. As I go over the staff I've seen in my head, I can't say I disagree with Laurel's assertion.

"Your sister had more liberties than me to roam around here and look for clues. The last time I saw her, she gave me a flower and this..."

Laurel hops off her bed, turns the cot over, unzips the bottom, and slides a stack of bits and pieces of paper out, with an envelope, which she hands to me.

I peek inside the envelope to find a note and a dried flower, unlike any blooms I have seen on the property. "Where did she get this from?" I ask.

"Well obviously somewhere here," Laurel says, pinching what looks like a torn off corner and sliding it to me. I recognize Annie's handwriting, although it appears a bit more mature since the last letter I read from her.

The places you'll go to find me
are not the places you need to look
to set me free.

"That's an odd thing to write," I say, shivers running up and down my back, recalling the many times now I have heard that very phrase. This feels like a game of hide-and-seek, but minus the fun and minus the game.

"She was desperate to find Marguerite," Laurel says.

"We both were. But then she left, said she had to go, and I got locked up." She pauses. "So you know, you really should be careful."

Laurel also says Marguerite isn't the only person who has disappeared, that others have disappeared since. Patients. "As you know, it's not like we really have family checking up on us here." Laurel spins her hair on her finger. "Me and Annie, we didn't think they were dead, the ones who disappeared. Annie used to say: 'they are here. I can feel it.' She had some theories, like tucked in paintings, or maybe in the trees."

Laurel shrugs. "I don't know. But I hear them sometimes too and I think they should be set free. Maybe you could finish solving the mysteries here with me. I can't help but think that although your sister had a plan to go, she is still here too."

My breath catches when I inhale, but I ask a question anyway. "What's different about her disappearance from all the others?" I ask. "If she had a plan to go and was packing her bags, even gave you a note and a flower, why do you think she is still here?"

Laurel eyes me. "I know we've already talked about a lot, but this might be the part where I lose you."

I feel my lips purse. "Just tell me."

Laurel swallows. "I hear her singing sometimes, and I think I also hear her screaming."

I don't offer up that I have been hearing screaming at night since my first night here.

Better & Worse

As much as I like them, my conversations with Laurel make things both better and worse.

Better, because I feel oddly validated.

Worse, because now I am having the same experiences as a patient who is deemed high risk and dangerous, and because if any ounce of what we talked about is true, it means there is a real possibility that not only is a killer walking these grounds, but also he or she may be responsible for my sister being turned to stone.

And as conflicting as my feelings for Annie are, I would never want anything bad to happen to her.

Insane

defined as a state of mind which prevents normal
perception; seriously mentally ill

Crazy
defined as mentally deranged
especially as manifested in a wild or aggressive way

Laurel
defined as both of these
and yet somehow
I relate to her and she relates to me.

Insane
as in watching stone move
and believing it

Crazy
as in believing that somehow a gem glowing
is my sister communicating with me.

If Any Of This

has an element of truth
then what Laurel said about danger
is probably true too.

And at this point
although my curiosity
is blown wide open
the most important thing
is for me to get out of here

safely.

I'm really not sure
how much more I can take
of the crazy.

Impressions

"What do you remember about Annie?" I ask Kit the next time I see him.

His shoulders drop, as he stares off. "She was so full of life. She was...she was special."

Ha. I can't disagree with that. But somehow I think my idea of special and Kit's are two different things. "Know anything about where she went?"

"Oh God, it's been a long time since she's been gone. Can't remember. Seemed kinda odd if I remember correctly though. Like, discharge hardly ever happens so when it does there's usually talk about it for a while before it actually happens. With her, if my memory serves me, she seemed to just make up her mind one day that she was doing something different." He laughs and looks at me. "Kinda like you, I guess, but she was an adult, capable of making that decision for herself."

"So you don't remember where she went? Did she tell anyone where she was going?"

"Honestly, I can't remember. It's been so long, but again, I'm just hired help. You would probably get more information out of one of the staff."

He stops again and looks at me. "She's your sister. Why don't you know where she went?"

"Long story," I say.

I Turn The Pendant

over and over in the palm of my hand
as I sit down on the ground
and lean against one of the concrete blocks.

Where did you go, Annie?

This piece of jewelry
is the only piece I have of her
and a couple years ago
even that would have been too much.

I rarely thought much about her.

I didn't see any other side of her
other than the side that caused such relief
when she left.

I wanted Mama to be okay
to have something left for me
once in a while.

I didn't understand my sister.

Never knew her.

When we stopped hearing from her
communication tapered off so gradually
I didn't think much of it.

Still I assumed she'd show up
to my graduation.

I expected I'd look out at the crowd
and see her there sitting next to Mama.

My thoughts that day
my audience scan for her
was disrupted when I heard "University"
after Pierce's name.

As I trace the outline of the flower
with my fingernail I feel a curiosity for
the girl Laurel knew
the girl Kit knew
something I have never felt for Annie.

Searching

In the garden, I take in each of the angels one at a time. *Speak to me,* I urge them, so terrified before, but now wishing they would communicate with me again. If Annie is here somewhere trapped on the grounds, I am going to find her, and the angels may have a clue.

But they are still today, cold and quiet.

When I get to the girl with her face in her arms, I squat down beside her, running my finger along her arm, pushing the dirt out of the crack in her bent arm. *Where did you go, Annie?*

An even scarier question is, if she is here against her will, is she even alive? I shudder at the thought. There is no way, right? It must be just this place and its depravity getting to me.

But if Marguerite was everything she is described as and someone killed her, would someone hurt Annie too? Is it a grave I should be looking for?

As I get to the statue's hair, pushing dirt caked in the carved waves, the stone starts to move, turning upward, and I lose my balance falling back, my palm smashed against the ground.

"Annie?"

It is undeniably her and she looks right at me before turning her face back into her arm.

Either I Am Losing Touch

with reality
or

Either I am losing touch
with reality
or

Either I am losing touch
with reality

or

or

or

Blackbird

Mama used to sing us a song at bedtime. Before Annie went to Shepley, she sang it to us together. We would pile up in her bed the three of us, and with one on each side, an arm around each of our shoulders she would sing.

Blackbird singing in the dead of the night...

Mama's voice is low and haunting, yet also soothing. Like Anne Murray. She would run her fingers through my hair while she sang, comb my eyebrows, caress the side of my face. It was impossible to keep my eyes open and I don't think I ever made it through the whole song awake.

I fall asleep tonight remembering the sound of her voice, and it stays with me into my dream. An odd dream of me, Mama, and Annie at the apartment, the last place the three of us lived together.

We are in Mama's bed and she's singing Blackbird, but this time me and Annie are singing with her. That never happened. That was the one time we could guarantee Annie would be quiet. When Mama sang.

But in my dream Annie and I are both singing along with Mama. And then Mama stops. So I stop. But

Annie keeps singing. And when I look over at her, Annie has tears running down her face, as she stares straight ahead blankly.

"Annie!" I say. But she doesn't hear me, just keeps singing.

I startle awake, jolted by how real it felt, and also so dreamlike at the same time. Annie. But when I sit up, the singing doesn't stop.

"Annie?" I whisper. I turn around in my bed, scanning the room, but there is nothing there. No one there. But Annie is here. I can feel her.

I reach for the necklace laying on the nightstand, craving comfort, and instead find that it is warm to the touch.

Wide Awake Now

I realize how strange it is to be awake in the middle of the night here when it is quiet. Because the singing continues so softly, it is almost inaudible. But free of screaming, I'm left to hear the moans, groans, and creaks of the castle that I usually only notice during the day when people are moving around. It somehow makes more sense then.

Now, in silence, I listen to soft quiet singing that must be my imagination. I can't help but wonder what these walls have seen and what this house is trying to say. The riddle Annie left with Laurel comes to mind.

The places you'll go to find me
are not the places you need to look
to set me free.

When I first read it, I assumed Annie was referring to herself. But if she was trying to leave and was stopped after giving the flower and note to Laurel, perhaps the riddle has nothing to do with her at all.

Perhaps it is actually a clue to Marguerite, a way of earmarking the book, leaving a spot for someone to pick it back up.

***

I must have eventually fallen back asleep because when I open my eyes again, warm bright light spills through the window. I overslept. Damn it. I pop out of bed, wondering why no one came to check on me. Or maybe they did but I was so far out of it that I didn't stir.

I recall my dream, recall Annie, and what I wondered about before is confirmed in my mind. Annie is part of the mystery of Shepley. I need to get back to the garden so I can talk to her.

The Worst of Timing

"Didn't learn your lesson, did you?" Kit startles me, and I jump and then settle myself back into pruning the rose bush next to Annie.

"What do you care?" I say.

"Nothing," he says. "I just thought you were trying to get out of here is all."

"I got in trouble for not following the rules, not 'cause they think I'm crazy." I turn to him and the grin on his face makes me want to smack him. "Not that it's any of your business, but it seems to be a regular occurrence that your nose shows up in my things."

"I'm just messing with you," he says, a little twinkle in his eye. "But for real, you probably shouldn't be talking to objects or yourself, whichever it was, if you want to get out of here. You never know who's watching."

I look around. "It's just me and Ronnie out here today and I don't think Ronnie cares."

"You never know," Kit says. "Either way."

"Well after my birthday, I don't have to stay, even if they do think I'm crazy."

"Not true," Kit says. "If they think you're a danger, they can keep you here."

No one told me that, but I'm not going to let on that his words sent an uncomfortable twist rolling through my stomach and ribs.

"Danger?" I scoff. "Me?"

"I don't know. The way you're holding those shears. I wouldn't mess with you."

I flip my wrist toward him, the sharp edge angled in his direction. "Yet, what do you think you're doing?" I joke, and he laughs, but like always it is the wrong moment because around the hedge appears none other than Feller.

"Well, well, Emily Jones, just can't keep your head out of trouble, can you?" Her smug smile makes me want to turn the blades toward her.

"It was a joke," Kit attempts.

"You," she says, turning to Kit. "Don't you have things to do? Or maybe you'd like me to tell Headmistress Harrison that you think it appropriate to flirt and frolic with the patients here instead of working your hourly?"

Kit gives me an apologetic look before turning to the hedge studying for anything I might have missed.

Feller grabs a hold of my arm, her fat fingers wrapping just above my elbow so hard I feel the mark coming on. "So you think it's funny. So you think it's all a game." She squeezes my arm like she's frosting a cupcake with it. "We're not here for your games, Jones. You're just like your sister, so stubborn, so hellbent on doing the wrong thing. Unfortunately Shepley just can't have that. We will straighten the stubborn spirit out. I will straighten it out if it's the last thing I do."

Comparison

I have been compared
to a lot of things in my life

A brat—by Mama's boyfriends
A hole—by the boy at school
A flower—by Pierce

But being told
I'm just like Annie, crazy Annie?
That's a new one.

And now that I think of it
I can't think of a single way
in which we are alike
other than maybe our looks.

This "stubborn spirit" Feller points to?

Annie was never like me.
Annie was sick.
Annie was unable to cope with life.

Mean in a rage, even dangerous.
But she was not stubborn.
She was not me.

Me, The Storm

I am hellbent on something—
that much is true
Being here has revealed a side of me
I never even knew.

But is it this place
or being away from him
that did it to me?
Taught me to care too much
and also not nearly enough
about anything & everything.

Mama used to say
what comes out when things are hard
is what you really are.

So what does that say about me—
that rules mean nothing?

That I do what I want
disregarding the consequences
that might come to be?

I guess I'm just a storm in motion
thundering after my own needs
zapping anything
that gets in the way—
You could call me
friendly neighborhood lightning.

I'm the storm
I'm the rulebreaker

"Perfect"
for so many years
and now, no more than a disastrous mess
hurricaning my way back
toward the one thing
that made me feel safe—

love.

The Office

I am sweeping on the sides of the carpets in the hallway, when Headmistress's office door flings open. "What is that awful...Jones. Of course. I shouldn't even be surprised."

I glance up at her. "Good morning to you," I say, and she looks at me like she wants to impale me with the broom, but then her face straightens and says: "Hurry up. I need a hand."

"Yes, ma'am," I say, sass undetectable. I get back to work, but she's tapping on her desk. "Any minute, Jones. Like I have all day."

"Yes ma'am," I say and I am actually a little bit afraid. I am also a little bit excited.

"Take a look at this for me, would you?" she says, as I walk into her office. "And close the door behind you."

My hand falls to the door knob, guiding it closed, but the slat is heavier than I expected and closes with a thump. I don't remember this from the last time I was in here, but my last visit to this room wasn't exactly permitted. I wait, and she motions for me to come closer.

"My eyes are not what they once were," she says, flipping a couple pieces of paper to face me. "I'm working on the seating for the ball. Usually there is not a lot of variance, but this year is anticipated to be our biggest year yet. I need to somehow fit extra seating and refreshment tables on the map, while still leaving space for the stage and the dance floor."

The chicken scratch map is hardly decipherable and doesn't seem to reflect what she is suggesting.

"Why not build around the stage and dance floor?" I suggest. "Start with the same basic idea you usually use but add the extra tables around the outside. That way it still feels the same to the guests but you are able to accommodate more people."

I want to look up, look around, take in whatever I missed last time I was in here, but I need this time with the Headmistress, so I force myself to stay focused. I glance up at her face which is still intent on the map, her wrinkles much more apparent up close.

"Yes, yes, I suppose you're right," she says, running a finger along her jaw. She stops, leans her chin on her pointer and looks at me, although it feels more like she is looking through me rather than at me. This interaction, nicer than every other encounter I have had with her up to this point, makes my skin and spine crawl with angst.

"Did I ever tell you your sister did that painting over there?" she sighs.

I refrain from the urge to tell her she wouldn't have had the chance and turn to face the wall she seems to be staring toward the wall with the door I entered through.

Covering the walls on both sides of the door and surrounding the door itself are dozens of pieces of art crammed together, almost stacked on top of each other they are so close, all housed in thick gilt frames.

"Which one?" I ask.

Headmistress pushes up and zips across the room, no sound accompanying her footsteps to an art wall on the right of the door. A large piece is the obvious center, clustered amongst many smaller frames.

This particular painting depicts what appear to be scattered bones in a desert, sand smatterings the primary story. The bones look like a mix of human bones and something else I'm unsure of. Most of the massive painting is composed of the same general hues, browns, whites, creams, tans. The only disruption to all of the monotony, is barely visible by size, but because of color and texture grabs my attention like a magnet.

Peeking from one of the half sand covered rib cages off the lower right side of the scene is a tiny lime green sprout, no bigger than the tip of my finger. It stands on end with what look like two little arms, stretching and reaching. The only sign of life, but so demanding of its space.

"Your sister was brilliant," Headmistress sighs.

Despite the dozens of unformulated questions and thoughts squiggling in my brain like globs of jello, the response I blurt is: "Was?"

"Is—" she says quickly. "Is." She sighs. "It's just...I haven't heard from her in so long. She left here somewhat abruptly. Took me by surprise the day I found her at the front door with her bag. I always hope my patients will keep in contact with me, you know, from time to time after they leave here, but your sister did not."

"Did she say where she was going?" I ask, more and more blobs attempting to squeeze into my brain, despite the space that was already not enough.

"No," she says.

I look at her out of the corner of my eye to find she is still staring at the painting. She sighs. "I had hoped you might know."

Bad Day

Some days I can take it.
Others I can't.

Can't see anyone
Can't do a thing without being watched
Can't even use a damn phone.

I miss Pierce.
I miss Mama.
I miss normal life, life outside of here.

Life where I'm not scared, sad
or both all the time.

And now this.

An undeniable feeling
that in addition to something being off here
my sister's "disappearance"
was no accident
or "discharge."

She was investigating a murder
and was halted by someone here.

That much I can say with confidence.

Then there's the unshakable feeling
that Headmistress knows something
about my sister
beyond what she let onto.

And I am scared.

One more creepy thing happens
and I'm out of here.

I can't do this anymore.

I'll take my chances.

I'm close enough to being an adult
it wouldn't be an issue.

I don't even belong here.
I'm not Annie.

It was all a mistake for me to come here.
It's not like I'm
actually crazy.

Sighting

But this time the plan I make in my head has to actually happen, because despite me thinking surely the creepy stuff is going to stop now that I've decided to do something, it doesn't stop.

For all the rumors about Marguerite being spotted from time to time, I have yet to talk to a single person who claims to have seen it. Not that I want to hear it confirmed, and not that I would necessarily believe it if I did. As the rumor goes, it happens at night, so I wouldn't be able to see it anyway, unless I snuck out of my room.

Tonight as I am sitting by my window, I see what looks like a torn piece of a cloth, fluttering in the breeze. I blink several times, and then decide I'm not playing and crawl over to my bed. A shattering sound covers my ears and I think for sure my window is busted.

But when I finally get the courage to unbury my face and look up, I spot the piece of cloth, splayed across my window, somehow sticking, translucent, other than a streak of red on the edge.

Plan

I'll take Kit's station wagon. It's right next door, and he probably keeps the keys on him, or in the car.

If he keeps them on him, that poses a challenge to figure out, but with any luck, he doesn't.

Once I have the keys, I'm out of here.

That will at least get me to town, and I'll figure out what to do from there.

I can't stay here anymore. Kit wasn't wrong. If I wasn't crazy when I first got here, I will be by the time I leave.

Luck

I'm assigned to work in the garden which gives me a chance to locate Kit's car. As I approach the messy overgrown shrubs dividing the two properties, I spot the car parked exactly where I need it to be.

I try really hard to not think about the fact that this plan only extends until I make it into town and that I'm going to have a hundred other things to figure out once I get there. One step at a time.

Right now I just need to focus on getting out of here safely. Get out of here, before I end up losing the rest of my fragile grip on reality.

Or like Annie, halted.

Or Marguerite, silenced.

The Necklace Presses Against My Leg

while I work
and I almost feel bad
for my escape plan.

There are clearly
some sketchy things going on here
and Annie, my own flesh and blood
is trying to make me aware
while I am peacing out of the madness.

I should feel bad.

This should be enough to stop me.

Wanting to find Annie
should matter most.

But I was never enough
for anyone else

so
why
stop
now?

More Luck Graces Me

Ronnie is outside working, which makes things a little more difficult initially because I can't just bolt for that side of the property. There's no reason I need to be over there on paper at the moment. Which leaves me no choice but to engage with him.

"Say there, Ronnie," I say, busying myself with weeding around the trees again. "How's it going?"

His eye is looking all around me or maybe right at me as he says: "Oh you know, another day. I'm getting tired, I suppose. It happens when you get to be old like me. One of these days, I'm going to need to retire."

"You? Retire?" I say. "Already?"

"I've been around since this place was born as Shepley, nearly about anyway. I reckon Sheila will have to find a replacement for me if I retire."

"Sheila?" I say, confused.

"Or I guess," he says, "Ms. Harrison?"

Headmistress. How strange to think of her as anyone other than the Headmistress. Sheila. Huh.

I approach the car and before I even make it to the door, I spot a rusty key ring hanging on the rearview mirror with two keys attached, one with the Ford emblem and the other looking more like a house key. Score.

I am so tempted to snatch them now, but I can't leave until tonight anyway, so it seems like a bit of a risk.

I make my way back through the brush, my legs torn up by the time I get back on the Shepley side of the property line.

Tonight.

Just a few more hours to make it through. After bed checks, I'll be gone. Safe. A lot could go wrong, but I have no other options.

***

But to my great surprise, a lot does not go wrong. In fact, it seems to go even smoother than I imagined it could have.

I wasn't allowed to bring anything here with me, so I have nothing to pack, other than an outfit change and some food I wrapped in napkins at dinner. Nothing appetizing, but it will hold me over.

I have the twenty dollar bill that I keep stitched into the side of my shoe for emergencies, and I'm sure I'll end up needing that, but not just yet.

Climbing out the window is risky, but with how many noises a single step makes in the house, I can't chance any other option.

I tie a piece of rope I found in the garden shed to the vent under the window. After checking the yard as thoroughly as I can, I ease the small canvas bag down, and then myself after.

The moon is shining bright tonight illuminating the big open lawn, so I dash for the first tree in the procession that line the driveway, and then make my way to the edge of the property weaving in and out of the trees.

When I finally make it through the shrubs and to the car, I breathe a sigh of relief to see the keys are still hanging on the rearview. I squeak the door open as slowly as I can, tossing the bag into the passenger seat, and barely closing the door behind me.

Kit's house is close enough that if anyone were looking out the windows right now, they would be able to see a figure in the car, but probably not make it who it is. If I can just get this thing started and on the road.

LOL, JK, Joke's On Me

I'm quick but not quite quick enough apparently.

The wagon starts up just fine, but the engine makes such a ruckus that a light in the house instantly flicks on. After a quick scan of the driveway, I shift to drive and floor it. I've come too far and at this point, I'm already caught, so I might as well make a last ditch attempt.

The front door of the house slams, and Kit comes running after me. I can't see clearly enough to speed up any faster because the lights are so dim, which ultimately gives him the chance to jump on the tailgate.

I don't stop.

He crawls across the top of the car, and despite my best efforts to weave in order to lose him, his grip appears to be solid because he manages to make it to the passenger door. He maneuvers it open and slides into the seat next to me, shutting the door behind him. I can tell that he is looking at me, but I just stare straight ahead, eyes focused on the road, pothole after pothole jarring my head.

"A little lovesick, a questionable grip on reality, and enough sass for a whole gaggle, check, check, check. But a thief? Didn't take you for that."

The driveway to his house dumps into the road that we turned off to go to Shepley that first day that feels so long ago now and I take a right heading toward town. One hand on the steering wheel, I reach down to my sneaker and start digging trying to rip the threads.

Kit grabs the steering wheel, putting his other hand up. "Whoa there, Em. Careful."

I realize what he's likely thinking and straighten back up, putting both hands on the steering wheel, still locked on the road ahead.

"Wanna tell me what's up?" he asks, watching me.

"Listen, I'll give you money," I say. "I have twenty dollars. Just drop me off at the end of the road and don't tell anyone. I don't want to cause any problems. I just need to get the hell out of here."

"You know I can't do that," he says.

"Well I can't stay here anymore, so you're going to have to figure something out because going back is not an option for me." My foot is heavy on the gas, as we roll toward the main drag.

"What's your plan anyway?" he says, and I don't dare tell him the truth, that I don't even have one, but that roughing it would be better than another day in this hell.

"Let me guess, your booboo Prince Charming is gonna meet you in town? Steal you away and solve all your problems?"

"I don't need Pierce to solve my problems," I spit, pissed at his implication. "I don't need anyone to solve my problems. I solve my own problems."

"Really?" he scoffs. "That's what you're doing right now, huh? Solving your problems by taking a risk like this that could land you somewhere worse than Shepley? Or worse, land you back at Shepley, but locked up with no freedom? You think it's bad now, you oughta try not being able to leave your room. Then you'd realize how good you had it, free to roam free to look at—whoa, Emily, watch ooouuutttt."

After the most awful crunching sound that nearly convinces me I just died, I squint my eyes open. "Where did that turn come from?" I say. "I didn't see that at all." I rub at my forehead, feel a bump forming, the smell of smoke overwhelming my nose and lungs.

Kit coughs an exaggerated cough, clearing his throat. "Are you sure about that? 'Cause I was starting to wonder if you're just generally a wrecking ball."

"Well, you could have just let me go and we wouldn't be having this issue right now," I scream. I push the door of the car open and pull myself out, slamming it behind me.

"I'm losing my mind, Kit," I say. "You said it yourself. Questionable grip on reality. I have to go. I can't go back there. You have to let me go."

Kit climbs out and walks around, following me. "Or, novel idea," he says, flipping his hands up dramatically.

"You could just suck it up, do your time for a bit longer, and get out of here the right way in a few weeks. Isn't your birthday coming up soon here anyway?"

"Not fast enough," I say. "You don't understand anyway. You don't know what I have to deal with here. You don't have a clue."

I'm walking faster now. I want him to just give up. He needs to just give up.

But he matches my pace and asks, "What is it? All the scary monsters?"

I don't respond. He's just making fun of me. My head is starting to hurt and I don't know what I'm going to do, but I need to figure this out.

He reaches out and puts his hand on my arm. "Let's just talk, Emily."

"No," I say. "I have to go. I have to get out of here. I can't do this anymore."

"Stop," he asserts, and for some reason I can't identify, I listen and plop down on a big rock on the side of the dirt road, and puff a big sigh out.

"That's probably the first time you've breathed in a few weeks for real, isn't it?" he says, sitting down next to me, and I can't say he's wrong. "Look, I don't live there so I know it seems like it's easy for me to say, but I promise you don't want the consequences of this. What do you have left, two months? You really can't suck it up and leave here with no stars after your name? Because I promise you, it can be a whole lot worse than it is right now."

I want so badly to tell him about my experiences, how I'm in danger and I'm going crazy but I know he won't get it and I really don't want to hear it right now. "It's just..." I say. "I'm not even supposed to be here and this place sucks and I'm sad all the time and I just don't want to be here anymore."

Kit shrugs. "As long as you stay focused on the picture in your head of 'supposed to', you're never going to move on." His words sting, and I just want the conversation to be over with.

"Look, I won't tell anyone," he says. "Let's go back. I'll cover for you. I won't tell anyone you tried to run away. Just don't do this. You'll regret it. I know it feels like a solution right now but it'll make things so much worse. Less than two months and you can be gone. I know you've endured for longer than two months before."

He doesn't know half of it.

"Start looking ahead a bit, Em. You can do this. Start making a legitimate plan for when you get discharged. That'll make the days pass." Kit stands up and starts walking back in the direction we came from, seeming to expect I will follow. "Besides," he says. "You kinda owe it to me at this point seeing as how you wrecked my car."

I fling angry tears into the dark. "I'm not coming with you," I tell him, as I take off running in the other direction.

He is at my side in an instant and puts his arms around me. "Damn it, Em. Stop. My dad already knows I'm out here with you. You won't make it."

"I don't know why you're so convinced that this is good for me," I say, flinging myself out of his grip. "You're an asshole for not just letting me go. What's it to you if I screw my life up? It's already screwed up."

Kit shrugs. "You're the only one who thinks that."

Kit's Fib

when we get back is laughable.

"Emily, here, she really spared my rear.
Sorry. But I was really in a pickle
and I don't know what I would have done
if she wouldn't have agreed to come with me."

It got me past the nurse
who was clearly eager to get
back to her bed.

She flaps her hand around
staring at the ceiling
about as much emotion in her voice as a snail.
"To your bed, Jones. See to it."

But as I walk past her
she flips the log open
and writes something
and I know there is going to be more
to deal with in the morning.

I Cry

in my bed.

Pissed
that I was so close to getting away, but didn't.
Again.

Resentful
that for whatever reason, Kit couldn't or wouldn't
just look the other way.

Despairing
that I'm not getting back to normal life
back to Pierce.

Uneasy
about what more is to come in the days ahead
now that my only way out is gone.

Investigation

Kit and I are both brought in for questioning. Headmistress talks to him first, then me. Unsure of what he said, I try to give as few words as possible. But Headmistress is eying me. "This sounds like utter tomfoolery, Emily Jones. Why were you really sneaking out of your room? And how did you manage to get out the front door?"

I don't dare tell her the truth because I don't want to be moved to a room with no window. "Kit needed help and I know it was against the rules, but what would you do, if you were me and someone said they needed help?"

Headmistress blinks owlishly at me. "So you were just so helpful that I should look the other way, right? Let this go because you were being a good citizen?"

"Exactly," I say, nodding.

"Mhmm," Headmistress says. "That's not going to happen. All of these infractions, with the period of time you have already been here? I would have thought we would have already broken you of trying to flee. Ah well. Some patients just can't be helped."

"I can," I say, desperately. "I know it was terribly irresponsible of me. I will never do it again. I promise."

"Clearly you didn't learn your lesson from getting sent here for a very similar behavior. What is it with you and running away?"

I know there's nothing I can say that she will believe so I just go back to pleading my case. "I truly am sorry, Headmistress. Please, just give me a chance to fix this."

"Oh, trust, I will," she says, tapping on her paper. "You will have plenty of chances to fix this, once you have done your time."

Kit is still standing in the hallway when I exit and he gives me an apologetic look which makes me even more mad. I make a face at him and then storm off without eye contact.

Screw him. He should feel bad.

I Heard About Yer Little Charade

Tilly says
tossing my breakfast through
the window in the door.
"Thought yew was gon'
have a roll 'n th' hay
wif th' boy, 'uh?"

"What?" I say
wondering how she found about it
and how much she knows.
"Ew, hell no. He needed my help
jump-starting his car is all."

Add to the already not plausible fib Kit started
especially seeing the car is wrecked now.

"Mhmm, sure.
Don't think yer playin' any tricks on me, Jones.
I ain't stupid."

Solitary Round #2

double the time
followed by Laurel duty.

As if it wasn't bad enough before.

I guess I'll never get
one of the lesser punishments I heard about
when I first got here
like toilet duty.

Admitted
my rule-breaking is on a different level
but still.

Why Kit wouldn't just let me leave
infuriates me.

If it weren't for him
I would be out of here.

Gone.

Maybe in Pierce's arms
this very moment.

But instead
I'm here
I'm in trouble
and I have no end in sight
other than a birthday
that might as well be a decade away
at this point.

Back To See Me So Soon?

Not that I'm complaining or anything," Laurel says.
"You're the most tolerable thing
about this place yet."

"Whatever would you do without me?" I laugh.

"I don't know," she says
and somehow
even though I know she is joking
I can't help but feel she's genuine
and actually enjoys
being around me.
"So what did you do this time?"

I sigh. "Tried to run away."

Laurel shakes her head, smirking.
"Sneaking into Headmistress's office
and running away. Damn girl.
You don't stop at anything, do you?"

"Apparently not," I say
though sometimes I wish I could.

Probably

        I

probably

        shouldn't
        share everything with Laurel yet.

        It's

probably

        too soon.

        I

probably

        should keep
        it to myself.

        But
        I'm

probably

        going
        crazy

        so what's the harm
        in telling?

And so I resign myself
spill every last one of my beans
to the only person here
who seems to get it.

Spilling My Guts

"I don't buy it, Laurel," I start with. "She's the one who did this to Annie. I know she is. She had Annie's necklace, for Peter's sake. She trapped Annie in that garden, along with all of those other people, and she lets people believe they have just moved on and left here. What I can't figure out is what the point of that interaction was. Why would she bring me into her office? An office which still, by the way, feels office-y. There was nothing about it that gave me any clues. I mean I suppose maybe the art itself carries clues. Probably does. But beyond that, there's nothing there. Why so much secrecy around a space that feels like the sanest part of this whole place? What other stolen tokens hide in that room?"

Response

Laurel listens intently while I flood her with my stream of consciousness, before landing on a single takeaway. "You stole the necklace?" she whispers. "You found something creepy as hell, belonging to your *sister* no less, and you came to the conclusion that you should just take it? Haven't you watched any scary movies? That's just not something you do when you find something. Hell, who knows what Headmistress will do with that information? And she'll know it was you because you got caught in her office. Good luck with that. If you didn't have a target on your back before, which was unlikely because you're Annie's sister, you sure as hell do now."

Penance

Part of my punishment for trying to run away is that I am only allowed to do indoor duties now. There are so many more tasks on the inside and the eyes and ears are busier here, keeping me on constant high alert.

The library seems to be the best out of any duty I have had yet. It is probably the only duty that doesn't leave my skin crawling, and not because it isn't creepy. Books line floor to ceiling, slanting inward, as if one book out of place would bring the whole thing tumbling. All of the books have gray binding, so they blend into each other like decomposing bodies.

Ancient questionable wooden ladders lean against creaking walls and the closer I get to the top, the more it seems likely I am not making it out of here alive.

Beyond the decayed air in the room, it reeks of something I can't put my finger on, and each step sounds like I am chiropracting someone's pelvic bone.

I am in here with one or two patients who might as well be braindead. They schlump along with the energy of two week old oatmeal plopping into the trash can, affording

me the opportunity to move one hand in a waving motion ,
pretending to dust with one hand while holding a book
with the other hand.

"Chairs, Jones," the smaller of the two oatmeal
lumps says.

"What?" I say, pretending to scrub at the cover of
Persuasion.

"The chairs. They have to be rotated."

I slide the book back onto the shelf and climb down
the ladder. Moving the chairs around causes dust bombs
the size of baseballs to explode into the room. The back of
my throat and eyes are burning as I cough, stumble my way
to the door and fling it open, leaning against the wall outside
the room.

Somehow neither lump #1 nor lump #2 follow and
I don't hear so much as a single cough from the room.
Further confirmation that there is more dead here than alive.

Grudges

I'm still mad at Kit when I run into him in the kitchen so I duck the other way, but of course he sees me anyway and can't help but say something to me. "Look, Em, I'm sorry. If it makes you feel any better, I got in trouble too."

I roll my eyes and toss a cup of dirty dishwater on him, soaking his shirt.

"Hey!" he says, pulling the material away from his chest, attempting to fan himself with it. "I would have thought me saving your ass would have earned me some brownie points."

"Saving my ass?" I snort. "You call keeping me here in this prison *saving* me, when you could have just as easily looked the other way? You and I clearly have different definitions of saving."

"Well I could have told them what you were doing and it would have been so much worse for you."

"So?" I say. "There were exactly zero reasons to bring me back here. So no, you did not earn any brownie points with me. And no, you did not 'save' me. You're an asshat, but seeing as how I don't have many options for friends around here, you're the more tolerable of the options."

Kit laughs. "I'm honored to make the friend cut, even if it's by a bare margin." Then he blinks, a hint of exasperation. "I get it, but it's not fair to be mad at me. It's not like you have the money to fix the damage you did to my car, Miss Twenty Bucks."

At this point, I just want to clang him upside the head with a frying pan. "I take back what I said about you being a friend," I say. Pause, then add: "I'll pay you back once I get out of here."

"Yeah, well, then I guess you oughta focus on getting yourself out of here, huh?"

Recurring Dream

I am stuck in the same dream I had of Mama, Annie, and me in Mama's bed, Mama singing Blackbird, us singing along with her, and then Annie continuing after Mama stops. But this time Blackbird starts to morph into Annie humming a melody from a book Mama used to read to us, *Old Rose and Silver.*

Annie hated the book because the guy doesn't get the girl until the very last page of the book. Annie would say: "What a waste of the other 200 pages."

Mama would say: "Oh, but Annie, it wasn't! They loved each other all along and that was the journey they were on. It's a tale of endurance."

In my dream Annie hums the melody, and then starts singing *La Vie En Rose,* another song in the book. Except I don't feel like I am dreaming. Half awake, half asleep, I reach for the necklace and find it warm as before.

After Scouring The Shelves Thoroughly

I am in a funk because *Old Rose and Silver*
is nowhere to be found.

My hopes that somehow Annie
was guiding me toward a clue in my dream
are dashed.

Unless it is somewhere else in the house
but I haven't seen books laying around
so that could be quite the task
if that's the case.

I am about to leave
after finishing dusting
when I see the book
on the bottom of the shelf
tucked in the far right corner.

I somehow missed it
but it is here.

I slide the book off the shelf
and after glancing around quickly
wrap it in one of my rags
and tuck it under my arm.

If there was any intentionality
behind her singing this song to me
I am about to find out.

Inside the book

taped to the
last page

distorting
the flow

of the papers

is a key.

Rusty and dirty

but
a
key.

I return the book to the shelf, not that anyone would notice it missing but not wanting to tempt the eyes and ears.

Just not before sneaking it up to my room so I can stay up all night, reading it again of course.

Comfort

Ever since being confined to the castle, nothing new has happened in the creepy side of things, other than what I have already experienced. I am so used to hearing screaming at night, I could almost sleep through it. Almost. But ever since Laurel suggested it is Annie, I can't block it out even a little bit, and it keeps me up, pacing my room, until I'm so tired I crash.

To cope with these long dark hours, I have become a pro at digging to the sweet spot in memories of me and Pierce.

If I think too recently, then I remember that night and wind up stuck in a mental loop, wondering what went wrong and when. Clearly he didn't come to the decision to do something different with his life overnight, so I wonder if there was a single thing I could have done that would have made him stay.

Which time that we were talking, snuggling, or dreaming, did he decide he was done? Was it all at once or a slow decision that formed over time? That thought trail can take all night and makes me really really sad and then this place is even less tolerable.

So the sweet spot is to dig back a bit before graduation was approaching, when we first started planning Michigan. Back then, things were just as much his dream as they were mine.

If I sit in that place, all the times we laughed about stupid shit and shared earbuds, listening to music, the night sucks a little less.

I'm there now, recalling a time I was in a grumpy mood. Pierce said *Hey, come here, Emmy,* took me outside and led me to an old rope swing, hanging from a tree.

Hop up, he said, and he pushed me on that swing until the swaying motion wiped every ounce of sour right out of my brain.

But tonight as I watch shadows from the branches outside my window dance on the wall in my room imagining us under that tree again, I'm jerked from the memory by what looks like claws erupting out of the shadows.

I know I am just overly tired and not actually seeing this, but it's unsettling enough I don't want to watch. I plunk down on the bed, curl up and pull the thin scratchy blanket over my head, waiting for it to go away.

But then I feel hands wrapping around my shoulders and squeezing, digging into my arms. I hold my breath hoping he / she / it will lose interest and go away.

And if I acknowledge it, then what? What does it say about me? That I'm crazy?

But he / she / it squeezes until I cry out in pain, and a voice that makes me feel like a beetle is crawling up my spinal cord says: *I will hurt you more than this.*

I pop up, flinging the blanket off my head. "Who?"

But the voice is gone.

I stare back at the wall where the tree branch shadows are still sweeping back and forth, no claws.

One Step Forward

Three back.

A clue
and then a warning.

A shove in the right direction
and then "whoa, slow down and be careful."

I just want to solve this
because I'm on ticking time
until my birthday

and more importantly
it seems like
my days of relative safety here
are numbered.

Preparation

"Listen up," Feller squawks, making an attempt at being authoritative, but sounding more like a chihuahua. "We have two and a half weeks until the ball, which means we are about to be busier than ever. Your work must be pristine. There will be no slacking. No talking. No dilly dallying. If I catch any of you taking breaks without asking, there will be consequences. Everything's divided up on the board, so get to work. Chop chop. Jones, see me after."

The residents slip away in their different directions and I stand and wait.

"You're on double duty," Feller says, creepy eyes glimmering. "For some reason, you're the only one who seems to get things done for Headmistress. But I need the garden taken care of too, and you seem to be the only one who can get anything done out there. Seeing as how I'm always catching you yimmer yammering with the boy next door, if you cut the flap, you should have plenty of time for both. Are we clear?"

"Understood," I say.

Then she reaches forward, grabs my arm and squeezes. "I'm not playing games, Jones. Hear me? One more screw up, and house duty becomes permanent."

A visit to the garden and a visit to Annie. Maybe between the two, I'll figure out where Annie is trying to take me with this key. I never thought I'd be this excited for anything to do with this place.

But at the top of the staircase, just before the long hallway that leads to Laurel's room, Tilly is waiting. "Sup wif yew?" she says. "Been avoidin' me?"

"No," I say. "But I'm on double duty now."

"Lucky f'r yew," she says, a smug smirk on her face. "One o'these days you'll le'rn yer less'n."

I've never really liked Tilly, but somehow I like her even less now, and feel like I need to watch my back.

EEEEMMIIIILLLYYYYYYYY

Laurel hoots when she sees me. "What'd you do this time? Phone, attempt to run away, not sure what could top that."

"Well apparently someone must have overheard our conversation last time about me being the best thing for you yet because they decided to assign me to your space, as double duty. We're getting ready for the ball, so they want me in the garden because I'm the only one that gets anything done out there, but they also want me with you."

"Well lucky me," she says, and smiles, and when she does, I find myself smiling too. "Catch me up," she demands, and I produce the key from my pocket.

Unfortunately, she doesn't have any ideas on what it might go to, or what Annie might be trying to guide me toward. "Like I said," she offers. "I'm pretty sure she had it all figured out, and that's why she was trying to get out. But I really don't know all the details of her last few days here."

I hoped talking to Laurel would help me figure it out, but even just saying it aloud somehow settles something. Helps me along in figuring it out.

"Do you know anything about any of the others who have disappeared?" I ask her. "I mean, I know you said before that other people would have a better sense of that, but can you remember what any of them looked like, the ones you did remember?"

Laurel sighs. "Nat. Nat was one of the loudest patients here. You would have liked her. She used to make Feller so mad because she would say whatever was on her mind all the time, no matter what. Me, her, and Annie used to make jokes and prank people sometimes."

"What did she look like?" I ask.

"She always had her head up so high. Like nothing could take her down. And this just...beautiful face."

"I think I found her," I say.

The Garden

After being stuck in the house, I am so excited to see the roses and Annie I almost do a dance. I feel the necklace in my pocket seeming to light up almost immediately. Maybe it's just my imagination, but it seems warmer the closer I am to her.

"We have a lot to do," Kit says, appearing at the entrance, pushing a large utility cart full of plants. "We have to get all of these in the ground with Ronnie being out."

"Wait, why is Ronnie out?" I ask. Come to think of it, it has been a few days since I've seen Ronnie.

"No idea," Kit says. "These things...happen."

"Not around here usually," I say. "Ronnie's been here forever. He strikes me as the kind of guy who never takes a vacation day."

"You're not wrong," Kit says. "Yeah, come to think of it, it is a little weird that he's not here now, isn't it?"

Weird indeed. A shiver runs down my spine. "Well anyway, we might as well get to work then. I'll take my half and you can take yours."

"Not a chance, buttercup," he says. "We have to do this together."

"Ugh," I sigh loudly. "Why?"

Parking the cart and tossing me a hand shovel, he says: "Because. I have things I need to talk to you about."

"If this is another stupid apology or more making fun of me, I'm not interested," I say, picking up the shovel. "What are we doing?"

"Headmistress wants these lining the hedges."

I look around for a minute. "That's going to take forever."

"Yep. So get busy." Kit smirks. "Or like someone likes to say, chop chop."

"One of her is enough for this place," I say.

We start on the far side of the garden, furthest away from the entrance, and after laying down the first couple in silence, me digging and him planting and covering, I ask: "So what did you want to talk to me about?"

Kit looks around for a second, then picks another plant off the cart. "Remember how you asked me if this place was haunted?" he asks.

"Yeah," I say.

"And remember what you were saying about the statues and how sometimes they seem like people?"

"Uh huh," I say.

"Well," he says, looking around again. "I think you're onto something."

"I bet you do," I say. "'Cause I'm a broke wrecking ball who owes you big time, right?"

He smirks, but then says: "I'm serious, Emily. These statues here... I know people say heat plays tricks on you but I'm pretty sure like I would bet money on what I've seen. They move. I've seen it."

"Huh," I say. "Sounds like someone needs medication."

"Let me help you. I want to figure out whatever you were thinking before."

And although his tone is more serious than any I've ever heard from him before, I'm just not ready to show him my cards yet. "Hey," I say, pulling the key from my pocket and tossing it at him. "Any ideas as to what this might go to?"

Kit catches it and turns it over. "Man, I haven't seen a key like this in a minute. Where'd you find it?"

"At your mom's house," I say.

"Well, my mom's dead," he says, tossing the key back to me. "So that's awkward."

"Damn, Kit, I'm sorry. I didn't know..." I trail off and feel like an asshat but I already said it.

After a few minutes of quiet have passed, he says: "It's been a long time, Everyone always says I look like her though. I guess that's where I got my wavy locks." He shakes his head, curls following the motion.

"She where you got your smart mouth from too?" I ask before I can stop myself.

"Oh no," he says. "That's all my pop. He's quicker than me too. He can out-comment me any day. My mom was the closest thing to an angel you can imagine."

A response almost flies, but I decide to stop the roll I'm on, and at least make an attempt at being decent for once. "I'm sorry, Kit. That sucks."

"Thanks," he says.

We have finished up all the plants on the cart and I offer to go with him to pack up the next load. "So," I say, as we walk. "Want to help me figure out what the key goes to?"

"That type of key only has a few possibilities that it could belong to, if you're sure it belongs somewhere here."

"I am," I say.

"Well, the only doors with those locks on it are doors to rooms within rooms. So storage rooms, closets, that sort of thing. But yeah, I can help you look."

My best guess is or maybe it is more of a hope is that if it was a room Annie was using she must have been accessing it with some sort of ease. Perhaps it would be helpful to share that piece with Kit but I need to figure out a way to, without spilling all the beans.

With More Liberties Than Me

and fewer watchful eyes focused on him
Kit is a decent participant in my endeavor.

Assigning the key to him
gives me a chance to talk to Laurel
and get her feedback
on whether or not to enlist his help on the rest.

At this point
my primary clue is the key
and then of course the very vague
secondary clues of the riddle and flower.

But having someone on board
who can roam
and doesn't have a deadline
they can't miss
would be helpful.

Trust

"Help me figure this out," I say to Laurel. "Kit has offered to help me, but I'm still figuring out whether or not I can trust him. Do you remember him?"

"I remember Kit!" Laurel says. "But he was more Annie's friend than mine, so I can't really vouch for him one way or the other, other than that she probably wouldn't have been friends with him if he wasn't trustworthy. I guess the worst case scenario is he is playing you and going to rat you out. Then you get locked up like me and don't have a guarantee of leaving when you turn eighteen."

"Bad plan," I say. "And not an option. I have to get out of here as soon as possible. So what's the best case scenario?"

"That he's not playing you and actually saw what you've been seeing and wants to help. Maybe he fills in all the missing gaps, lessening your chances of getting caught and restricted to the house again?"

"Think they'd restrict me to the house when they need my help outside? Think anyone is even around to notice right now?"

Laurel shrugs. "You would know it better than I would, but I guess it really comes down to, can you trust Kit or not?"

When I think about it, my biggest reservation about letting Kit in is that I haven't forgiven him for not letting me run away. Sure, I stole his car and that was kind of a jerk move. And wrecked it. Also a jerk move, even if it was an accident.

But if he would have just let me get away, I would have left it in town, and he could have had it. I guess he didn't have any way of knowing that, but I'm still mad at him for it.

He was the first one to tell me the rumors about Marguerite and said there is room for things to linger around here so he can't be that closed off to the possibility. Plus, I've never told him about what I've seen in the garden so he must have actually seen it for himself.

The worst case scenario is a big risk though. My mind starts to wander thinking about Pierce and tears burn my eyes. I have to get out of here and nothing can get in the way of that. I can't allow anything to.

But at the end of the day, I don't mistrust Kit. He makes me mad a lot and I want to smack him most of the time, but I really don't think he is spiteful or the type to bait me, just to try to get me in trouble. I guess I'll see how he does on figuring out what the key belongs to and let him earn his way in.

It Is Almost Supper Time

marigold sunshine falling through the hedges
to rest on angel faces.

Annie has turned her face
and is propped on her arm
watching Nat and smiling.

"How do you do that?" I ask Nat.
"When I first got here you barely moved.
You didn't speak.
And now you're practically dancing."

Her hand moves to her mouth
as she puckers, while closing one eye.

"How, after years of being stuck
does it feel to move again?" I ask.

But her eyes drift to gaze beyond me
and I turn.

The couple is swaying side to side
the slightest of motion
but certainly moving.

The hard, cold mass in my chest
starts to shift
as I watch them smiling
and staring at each other.

I don't have enough room
for the warmth that presses
at the ache in my ribs.

It pushes
and flutters
and wiggles
and I want to join
in the dancing.

Dancing.

Not something
I have done
or even wanted to do
in a very long time

but now I do.

Leverage

As the house bustles with preparation for the ball, I feel less worried about eyes and ears, except I keep bumping into Tilly and she isn't friendly, like she used to be. Not that she was ever friendly, but now there's something else about her and I don't like it. The last thing I need is her watching me.

"Hey," I say to her, next time I see her. "Want me to take your hallway duty?"

Tilly's eyes narrow. "What's it t'yew?" she says, staring suspiciously.

I force my brain to come up with something that might add some humor. "Nothing," I say. "Just trying to crawl my way out of Feller purgatory."

She makes her best attempt at keeping a straight face but a crooked smile slips out anyway. "Alright, fine." Then her eyes lighten. "Does this mean we tradin'? I'll be in th' garden wif th'boy?"

I need her occupied, but her crush on Kit? Even better. There is only one final loop to close with this.

Kit is not impressed with my plan at all. "So basically you want me to distract Tilly so she'll stop following you around while you go try not to get caught looking for some stuff that you won't tell me about yet because I haven't earned my way in. Got it."

"The worst that happens is you end up having to kiss Tilly," I shrug. "You'll be okay."

"Thanks for renting out my mouth, Em. So generous of you."

"Sharing is caring," I remind him. "We've been over this."

"All I can say is, it better be good whatever you're after."

The Search

Tilly being distracted makes things easier and all the other patients and staff are too busy to notice much, affording me the opportunity to do a meticulous search of the two places I think I might find something.

First, I head toward the fountain so I can scour the space and surrounding areas. Although that goes against the clue line "the places you think" it makes sense to me that I would at least find something there if that is where Marguerite is spotted from time to time.

Something feels different about the space since I was here last, and I can't put my finger on it, until I realize there's a large almost statue-like rock, although it doesn't have the appearance of a person, at least not in the way that the ones in the garden do. This one looks more—rugged somehow, more—oh. Oh. Ronnie.

What have you done? I whisper, but the stone is still, any recognizable facial features concealed by moss.

Remembering

I'm frozen in place, and it takes me a few seconds to remember what I was doing. Searching. Right. Searching for clues.

But other than a few cigarette butts and this—Ronnie—there's not much of interest, and none of the eggplant colored calla lilies, so I head toward the house. I have enough time left to circle it slowly.

When I come up dry there too, I am at a loss. This leaves the back garden and the swamp beyond, unless it is somewhere inside, but that seems unlikely to me. An indoor garden? I guess it's a possibility, but I can't imagine anything could stay alive in there.

Getting to the back garden will mean crossing a large wide open space and sneaking around in daylight isn't exactly easy. It will have to wait until the ball when everyone is occupied for several hours.

Dress

"I need another favor," I say, relieved when I see Kit, a welcome break from my unsettling discovery. "I'm going to need a dress."

"Psh, you have a couple weeks til you leave."

"Not for that. I'm going to the ball."

Kit's eyebrows shoot up. "You aren't afraid of anything, are you?"

"I've never been to a ball and I'll probably never get a chance after this. I'm not missing it. Besides, it's a masquerade ball, so it's not like anyone will recognize me. So where are we going to find me a dress and a mask?"

Kit runs his hands through his hair. "Uh, there's a place in town we could try, I guess."

"You mean *you* could try," I say.

"Uh uh. No way in hell I'm going dress shopping for you without you."

"Uh, have you seen where we are? No way in hell I'm getting out of here for the day."

Kit smirks. "I might have an idea."

Guess

"I'm with Kit on this one," Laurel says. "You truly do not stop for anything."

"Oh come on, Laurel. Fess up. You want to go to the ball too."

Laurel sighs. "Ya know, it's kinda hard being me. On the one hand, the idea of getting dressed up and going somewhere like that sounds great. But on the other hand, I get frightened so easily by large crowds and lots of interaction like that. And also what would I wear?" She pulls at her uniform. "This is all I've been wearing for years, you know."

"Well, I could bring you something."

"It's not just that, Em. Also, look at me. Can you see me in a dress?"

"Yeah," I say, then offer: "I could find you a suit?"

"It's not even that," she says. "I'm that in between, you know? Can't really see me in a dress, but I can't really see me the other way either. So just like the rest of me, I don't really fit in anywhere."

Unsure of how to answer, I change the subject and tell her I didn't find any flowers.

"Well where did you look?" she asks.

When I tell her, she laughs. "Uh, hello, the riddle. Why would you think you would find it at the fountain?"

"Because of Marguerite," I say. "And just...I don't know. Didn't seem right to not at least make a pitstop."

"But if it's not the place you would think, then convenience shouldn't be coming into play here."

"Yeah, but you'll never believe what I did find there," I say, and I tell her about Ronnie.

"No way. No way!" Laurel exclaims. "What could lazy-eyed Ronnie have done to make Headmistress want to freeze him here? Oh, you were right. About all of it. If you needed any more evidence, this is it."

"And yet, somehow it doesn't make me feel better," I say. "Have you ever seen a baseball cap shaped stone? It's not exactly—pleasing."

"Come on, Annie," I say, as if she can hear me. "Give us another clue. Why did you make it so difficult?"

"Has Kit made any progress with the key yet?"

"We know a few rooms it doesn't go to," I say. "And I've nudged him toward the easier to access ones to start with. He can make a repair excuse for any room, so if he gets caught, it's not that big of a deal, but I still don't want him to get caught. Also if I am kinda jealous that his job is more fun than mine right now."

I Make Kit Swear

that he won't go into whatever room the key ends up being a fit to without me. But it backfires on me when he finally finds the room and won't show me where it is, unless I let him go in with me. Unsure of what Annie is leading me to, I'm wary, but he did prove to be useful, and I guess I can only put him off for so long.

"But we have a problem," I say. "Tilly. She can't see us sneaking around together or she's going to follow us. Our only option is one at a time."

Kit eyes me suspiciously. "You know, Em, I feel like it should be obvious by now that you can trust me."

I blink at him, and then say: "Fine." Give him the skinny on the note Annie left for Laurel and the key being from the book but leave out the parts that make me sound psycho.

"Whoa, this is like—big stuff."

"Shut your face and go keep Tilly busy. She better really believe you too."

"I like how it has become my job to take one for the team with her."

"Boohoo, my name is Kit and I don't like attention from girls."

"Exactly!" Kit says, missing or ignoring my sarcasm. "At least not girls like her."

"Well suck it up, because we need her not focusing on me."

"Yes ma'am."

The Room

A storage closet in an unoccupied room, two doors down from the room I stay in.

The door to the room is unlocked, but left closed, so I look left and right before sneaking in and closing it behind me as gently as I can. The room is bigger than mine, but sparse and untouched.

A scad of questions flood my brain, as I insert the key into the lock. How did Annie discover this room? Was it her room? How did she get the key? What am I about to walk into? What if it is all in my head and not Annie? Could it somehow be a trap?

I turn the key anyway.

Natural light seeps in from the bedroom, enough to illuminate the closet, revealing a metal chain, hanging from a light. Bracing myself for I don't know what, I pull the string. The light turns on.

Plain white sheets, grayed by dust, cover what appear to be what I assume are frames or artwork of some sort stacked against each other. There's not much else to the room yet but I close the door behind me anyway, so I can take a look.

I didn't even really know Annie painted until Kit mentioned it when I first got here. Like I'm not sure I have even a single memory of her painting. Maybe they aren't all hers. Maybe this room is a collection of art from other patients. I start with a stack to the right side of the room.

It seems to be nature stuff mostly: flowers, landscapes, animals. Her style is recognizable, these paintings clearly done by the same person who did the one Headmistress has in her office.

I move to another pile closer to the back of the room. The first one in the collection shows a building. I don't know if it is me trying to connect with it, or having some faint hint of recognition too far in the back of my brain to put anything together in a meaningful way, but I can't seem to make it any clearer from thinking about it.

Following the building, is a portrait of a park, bright green grass, and a playground with a rusty seesaw. Then there is what appears to be a living room in someone's house, and behind that, a portrait of an empty picture frame on top of a dresser. These seem to be telling some sort of story, but I'm not sure what yet.

I jolt when I flip to the next one. Bold, block letters, not scrawled in Annie's handwriting, but almost scratched in desperation covering the entire canvas. The words are all in black and then smeared, blotches of red and black smattered across the rest of the canvas.

OUCH.

DON'T CRY.

OUCH.

IT'S A GAME.

IT'S OUR SECRET.

SHH.

YOU LIKE THAT?

OUCH.

OUCH.

Nauseated to a point of feeling like I'm going to lose my lunch, I crumble onto the floor, holding my side. Annie was abused, and here all this time, I thought she was just crazy.

My brain is peppered with questions, but over the questions, is a thick layer of guilt. I feel like I invaded her safe space. She brought me here, I have no doubt of that, but this particular story wasn't why. She was guiding me to clues. I stand back up and lay the sheet over the paintings.

I don't want to start another, but I know I must, so I cross the room and start on the opposite side. This set starts with Marguerite. I recognize her from the portrait in the front hall, her brown skin and round eyes. I'm surprised Annie kept this one and didn't give this to Headmistress to put on display somewhere. It is beautiful.

The next one is of a little girl, I'm guessing Marguerite, based on her facial features, standing in front of the fountain out front. How did Annie paint Marguerite as a little girl? She didn't even know her at that time in her life. I think of the last progression, and I guess she must be trying to tell a story. Establish the characters first.

The next portrait is of Feller, younger, much younger than she is now, with Marguerite. They are in the library, posing as if for a portrait, but neither of them looks particularly happy or comfortable.

The next is of them outside again, facing off, almost like in a battle, both with their hands up. One with Feller, her arms crossed over her chest. One of Headmistress, hugging both of them one on each side.

The next seems a bit out of place, showing a little girl, perhaps Feller, standing on the steps of Shepley with a big brown suitcase.

Then a family portrait: Headmistress, Marguerite, a man, darker brown, than Marguerite but same eyes, and Feller. In this one, they all look happy. Headmistress is smiling, something I don't think I've ever witnessed.

A knock on the door thrusts me back to the present moment, and I drop my key, heart racing. "Em, it's Kit. Just wanted to check on you."

The door cracks open and I start pulling all the sheets back up. I have no idea how much time has elapsed, but it feels like it has been years, and I'm totally lost.

He puts his hand on my arm. "You alright?"

"Yeah," I say.

Things I Want To Say To Annie

1. I'm sorry
2. I didn't know
3. You had so much to carry
4. It wasn't your fault
5. I hate that you went through that
6. I hate that I've hated you
7. I wish I could go back and not hate you
8. I feel guilty for hating you
9. Can we try this sister thing again?

Fortunately

I don't have to wait long for an opportunity to go back in, leaving me almost no time to process what I saw. I do my best to block it all out on the right side of the room, even though I know it is a risk Annie took when she chose to lead me in here.

But the rest is more confusing. She seems to be telling a story about the relationship between Marguerite and Feller and I'm not sure what significance that has. I find my spot in the stack again remembering Marguerite's dad, who I have never heard mentioned and never seen.

The one following that is of Marguerite and Feller holding hands like they were playing ring around the rosy, although they are too old for that near a gazebo.

I'm not aware of any gazebos here, so I'm not sure where this was supposed to take place. The next seems to jump forward in time because Feller looks more like what she looks like now. Marguerite is standing in a bedroom, holding a dress, and Feller is at the doorway, looking in. Kinda creepy. Just like her.

And then the pace suddenly changes because it is Marguerite and Feller at the fountain and Marguerite is wearing a white dress. Feller is behind her holding a dagger.

The next one depicts Feller stabbing Marguerite with what appears to be a large kitchen knife, blood spraying from Marguerite's chest and a look of terror on Marguerite's face. I barely stop to take it in, thinking surely it can't get more disturbing.

The next one shows Headmistress standing in the garden, holding her hands up and what appears to be bolts of electricity streaking from her palms.

This only kind of makes sense to me. It is confirmation of what I had already suspected, although I wasn't sure who was responsible. But how would she have convinced them to just stand there, so she could cast a spell and freeze them in time? There has to be more to it than just that.

And further, I can't help but wonder, why did she want them to stay?

Locking The Door

behind me
and slipping out of the bedroom
I close that door behind me
my heart racing.

I slip down the hall, realizing
I have completely lost track
of every logical thought in my head.

All of the warnings
make sense.

No wonder Annie
became in "such a hurry"
to get out of here.

An even greater urgency to leave hits me
as if it was not bad enough before.

The night of the ball I need to be ready to go
because if Kit and I are able to find the bones
I'm convincing him to take me
to town that night.
He won't say no to reporting this
and getting her taken away.

I need to play it safe
between now and then
because there is no other time
I would be able to search
without my absence being noticed.

With this bargaining chip
and any luck
I'll be able to convince Headmistress
to set my sister and the others free
and then I'll be out of here
and Marguerite will finally
be laid to rest.

I reach in my pocket
and squeeze the necklace.
I'm coming for you, Annie.
I'm setting you free.
Just hang on a little bit longer.

I Bump Into Kit

on my way into the kitchen
to help with dinner prep
after spending the rest of the afternoon
on hallway duty.

"Hey, hurry up.
I got permission from Headmistress
to take you to town to do
the other pickup but we have to hurry.
They're about to close."

As excited as I am
to get out of here for a few hours
I can't believe he managed to pull this off.
"What about Tilly?" I say.

Even though I don't particularly want
to be around her, I also don't want her
getting jealous and starting to follow me
around again. She has finally
started to leave me alone.

"Oh, I got her busy with something.
She'll be fine."

My stomach turns
and I feel like I shouldn't
leave without her
but not having her along
will make dress shopping easier
and I'll certainly
have more fun without her.

Town

The front end of the station wagon is still messed up from the wreck, but it runs, and gets us away from Shepley, probably just slightly faster than running would.

Having just finished the hallway in record time, sweat drips down my back soaking through my shirt. I wipe my face on my t-shirt, moaning about how hot it is, the wind blowing through the windows not doing the slightest bit of cooling.

"You could use a—" Kit reaches down, and next thing I know, I'm dripping with a cup of ice water he tosses on me. "Better?"

I'm laughing and he is too as he hits the gas and gravel rolls, poofing dirt and dust in my face.

He flips the radio on and I realize how long it has been since I've listened to music. Classic country station playing Johnny Cash and I sing along.

Swinging a left onto the main drag with a clattering sound that makes me wonder if the body of the car is about to disassemble, he pulls off almost immediately kicking up more dirt and dust.

"It's this close?" I ask. "I totally could have walked."

"Nah, we just gotta do this real quick."

Dottie's

A little mom and pop shack
an old lady with a boat hat serving
ice cream cones

cool, refreshing
on my tongue

melting and dripping
down my hand

and for the first time
in a long time
I forget

I'm
sad.

Lottery

Kit drops me off to get the dress, even though I offer to help with plants and then shop.

"Are you kidding?" he coughs. "I don't want to go dress shopping with you any more than you want my opinion."

"Well I don't want your opinion at all, but I'm a delight to shop with."

"I bet you are."

The Opportunity Shoppe smells less like opportunity and more like 80's desperation, but there's a dollar rack, a half off rack, and enough leather and tulle to give me hope of something that fits my style and price range.

A woman wearing a denim mini skirt and a cherry red cap sleeved t-shirt a size too small is propped on a barstool behind side by side glass cases of costume jewelry. The name tag that's pinned nearly to her armpit reads Candy with a squiggly Y, accentuating the cleavage pouring out of the split down the front of her shirt..

"What can I do for ya, darlin?" Candy drawls in a raspy voice, setting the Cosmopolitan magazine down, splayed open to save her spot, sucking a drag off the Marlboro in her other hand.

"I'm looking for a dress," I say. "Like a prom dress. Something fancy."

She cocks her head to the side and bright blue eyes no one could miss register confusion. Something tells me befuddlement is a normal occurrence for Candy. "It ain't prom season, sweetpea, but all the fancies are on that rack over thar. Expensive ones are closer to the fitting room in the back. Let me know if ya need any help."

I skip over to the first rack and start my process by dragging a hand across the materials. Some soft, some scratchy, some silky, some velvety. I make my way through, until one dress in particular stands out from the rest.

It is on the expensive rack, but I decide to try it on anyway. Between the overflowing wobbly rack and the size of the dress, it takes nearly an act of God to get it into my arms so that I can carry it to the fitting room.

I pull the curtain shut and slide out of my shorts and shirt before stepping into the dress, heaving to pull it over my shoulders. I grasp at the zipper with an awkward reach.

The dress is a stunning pink with puffed sleeves that are bigger than my head, a bow the size of the chandelier at Shepley, and enough material in the ruffles to decorate the entire castle. The best part of all is, to my utter delight, it fits me like it was made for me.

I slip back into my clothes, gathering the poof of material in my arms the best I can and make my way to plead. "Do you offer any discounts?" I ask Candy.

She exhales a drag, then asks: "What were ya lookin' at, darlin'?"

I floof the dress across the counter and pull the $20 out of my pocket. "I only have this."

She stares down at the dress and then says: "Oh geez, that old thang? Bless your heart. It's been here for years. I doubt it'll ever sell. You can have it." She eyes me like my taste in dresses is even more questionable than my appearance, and then says: "Tell ya what, I'll throw in some earrings for ya too."

I leave my money on the glass, scoop the dress and earrings up, and skip out of the shop. Kit shakes his head when he pulls up on the curb and sees me.

"Shut your piehole," I tell him, as I climb into the car, pushing the bag into the backseat. "I already told you I don't want your opinion."

"Wasn't planning on giving it," he says.

The Way Back

I tell him everything, about the angels, about Annie and the necklace, about the paintings, and my plan to use it all as a bargaining chip with Headmistress, once I've located the evidence, whatever Annie is leading me to.

"I can't believe you kept all that to yourself this whole time," he says. "Even when I first brought it up to you, you didn't tell me."

"Well, I had Laurel to talk about stuff with too. Besides, I wasn't sure if I could trust you."

"Laurel the one who got locked up for saying there was a murder?"

"The one," I say.

"Psh, you thought you couldn't trust me."

"Well," I remind him. "You have been the reason I've gotten in trouble multiple times now."

"Uh, I'm not nearly as gifted as you are at landing you in pickles. You do a pretty good job on your own."

He has a point, but I punch his arm anyway. "So my plan is to look the night of the ball while everyone is busy. You in on helping me?"

"Well I am expected to go to the ball as being on staff," he says. "But the best thing is the masks. So I should be able to sneak off with you, no problem. And then what?"

"Hopefully we find the body and can report it all and she'll be locked up for good," I say.

"God I just can't believe she did that. Marguerite was the sweetest person. Headmistress is going to have Feller's head.

Kit's Question

When we return, the sun is almost starting to set, but we have to get as much planted today as possible, so we start working immediately. Tilly meanders her way around the corner, glaring at me, but as soon as Kit turns, she smiles. "'ey," she says. "Was jus seein' if yew was needin' my help... or what..."

"Oh, Tilly," Kit is quick to jump in. "You worked so hard earlier. I wanted you to have a break. Emily here is always slacking so Headmistress wanted her to pick it up out here. Put her to work and straighten her out."

Tilly preens at his compliment, says: "Yeah, well, I *am* awful tired."

"Go take yourself a nice long shower," he says.

She smiles at him and says: "See ya tomorro'," then turns and slips back to the house.

"You're disgusting," I say to Kit. "Also, me? Slacking?"

"You told me to cover for you so I am!"

"Not at my expense, jackass."

We continue to work, and after a few minutes have gone by, he says: "So..." and just by the tone in his voice, I can tell the conversation is about to shift in a different direction. "You turn eighteen in a couple weeks you'll leave here and then what? Gonna go find your boyfriend?"

"Something like that," I say.

"Aww," he croons. "Is he going to meet you at the gates and sweep you away?"

"Not this again," I sigh, and at this point, I'm exasperated. "Are you capable of being mature for two seconds?"

He straightens up, and I clarify: "Also, well, I have to find him first. We're not technically together right now."

"Well yeah, seeing as how you tried to run away together and you're here and he's not, obviously there's something up with that." He stops and scratches his head. "Also, really? You stole my car to run away that night and you didn't even have a plan? With all your confidence, I thought for sure you would have had it made if I hadn't caught you."

I feel my shoulders drop and I want more than anything to lay down in the mulch.

"So you're going to go find him, convince him to get back together, and then what? Run away with him since you'll be an adult now and it'll be legal?"

"I wish it were that simple," I say, and, against my better judgment, start to explain.

Never

"Wait, wait, wait, let me get this straight." Kit has his hands
up. "He told you it'll *never* be and you still think it's
something? He said never? He actually said that, that you
will *never* be together, and you're still hoping?"

"Well we didn't get to finish the conversation," I
snap, pissed that of course Kit chose to focus on the one
thing he could hurt me with. "I left and stuff, but that
wasn't the only thing he said. He also said maybe like down
the road, after he graduates or whatever. He said he doesn't
know where life will take him and he has to see so nothing is
said and done."

Kit shakes his head, tilting the wheelbarrow to even
out the mulch. "Never is a pretty strong word to just, you
know casually, throw out there. Kinda sounds like you're in
denial, Em."

"I'm not in denial," I say, my voice less steady than
before. "We can figure it out."

"God, Emily. Grow up." Kit flings another scoop
of mulch into the bed. "Maybe if you put all that energy
into yourself instead of missing him, you would have some
insight into why you can't let go of someone who has clearly

left you behind."

Bubbles are wiggling and squirming in my head across my eyebrows and in my ears. "Well since you're such an expert on love, where's your princess, huh?" I say. "Since you seem to know everything, why are you alone?"

He doesn't answer my question, just turns the focus back to me. "Has it ever occurred to you that if he wanted to be with you, he would be?"

"Stop trying to be a subject matter expert on my life," I say, beating at the garden bed, the palms of my hands filthy and angry. "You don't know anything about Pierce."

But Kit doesn't stop. "He didn't say he was confused, Em. He didn't say he wasn't sure. He said never."

And I wince like I do, every time I hear the word. "Why do you keep focusing on that?" My voice cracks as I turn away, to hide the tears forming in my eyes.

"Maybe a better question is, why don't you?"

***

When I finally crawl into bed, despite the physical exhaustion and pain that course through my body, I cannot mute or even dull all the thoughts in my brain.

Annie. How did I never consider she had her own truth? All that time growing up I spent hating her, but she was a victim too.

And Marguerite's death. Will I find her? Will she finally be laid to rest? Can I stay safe in the meantime? Will I be able to convince Headmistress to set Annie and the others free? Who helped her? Now that I went to town with Kit and left Tilly here, is she going to start watching me again? Has she figured anything out?

And then Kit and this conversation. As much as he pissed me off in saying what he said, I have to admit, I don't have a plan. I've been so focused on Pierce, how to call him, how to get to him, what to say when I get to him, that not once have I thought about what I'm going to do or where I'm going to go, if he says no.

A quickly approaching birthday, adulthood within reach, a normal life on the horizon, if I grab for it, but how can I leave, with so much unresolved mystery?

And now the time of night has come where all that is on my mind is the one I thought I'd be beside, trying to settle how everything came untied that fateful world shifting night.

After Pierce & I Flipped Our Tassels

walked the walk
cheered, screamed, hollered
it was off to the graduation party.

I couldn't wait.

Just a few more hours, maybe even less
and we'd be on the road.

"Pierce and Emily against the world,"
I said, tossing my cap in the backseat
and rolling the window down
letting the wind blow through my hair.

Life was about to begin.

But that's when he started saying it again.
"There's something I need to tell you, Emmy."

"Why did you put down university?" I asked him.
"You hate studying.
That was never part of your plan.
Why would you tell the school that?"

He reached over
and slipped his fingers through mine.
"Em, listen."

But I didn't listen. I didn't want to.
"That's dumb, Pierce," I told him.
"And you're a twat
for making me look like a loser.
Plus it wasn't what we talked about."

And then he stopped the car.
We were driving down the street
through his mom's neighborhood
and he just stopped, put it in park
turned and looked at me.
"Emmy."

I told him I didn't want to hear
what he had to say
yanked my hand out of his
pushed the door of his car open
slammed it behind me
and took off running.

"Emily!" he shouted out the open window.
"Come on. We can still go to Michigan.
We'll take a few days. Spend it there.
Spend it together. I don't start school til the fall."

"Screw you, Pierce," I screamed at him
ran the five blocks home.

Hours later
I reached for my phone
and texted him.
Can we talk?

He texted back
said he was at the after party.

I freshened up
wiped the streaked mascara off my face
and changed my clothes.

If college was what he wanted
we could figure it out.

I didn't want to hold him back
from his dream.
I just didn't know that was his dream.
I thought *we* were his dream.

But we could work through it.
I was sure of it.

When I got to the party
he kissed me and handed me a drink.

"Quite the night already, but I missed you.
I'm glad you're here."

I told him I didn't want to talk there
in front of everyone
so we went and sat in his car.

"Why didn't you just tell me
you changed your mind?" I asked him.
"I would never hold you back."

I remember he took my hand then
and I started crying.

"We can figure it out," I told him.
"Screw Michigan.   It's just us.
I'm here for you."

"Emmy," he said.
"Emmy, you know I love you.
You know Michigan was what I wanted.
But I have to move on with my life
and let you go. It'll never be."

"Please don't do this," I pled.
"Please."

And then Pierce said:
"Maybe in 4 years.
I don't know. Who knows.
I don't know where I'll be
where you'll be.
I just don't know, Emmy girl
but I can't do this. Not now."

And from there
it just kinda goes hazy.

I remember finding mom's car
being grateful for her bad habit
of leaving the keys in it
because this once, it was convenient.

I remember starting it.
Planning to take off.

Disappear.

And that's about it.

I'm Crying Again

and I feel stupid.
I hate crying.
And more than I hate crying
I hate feeling responsible for it.

Why couldn't I have just ignored Kit
stepped aside from a conversation
that I haven't had with anyone
let alone someone who
consistently irritates me?

I'm sad
and I'm mad
and confused
and would give anything
to stop my brain.

All that time Pierce had
to say he was considering other options
but instead he stayed quiet
until he had already made up his mind
and then he left.

And every time I think I can forget
he is all I remember.

And that's the thing about grief.

You can never get away from it
never quite escape it.

It crashes against you
long after you have tapped out.

When you don't have anything to give
it eats you alive
bite by bite
until you disintegrate
and then it scratches at the dirt
you've sunk into
tearing after any lingering specks of flesh
still hungry
long after there is nothing left.

Grief is insatiable.

The Worst Night

As if it can't get any worse, it does, because just as I start to drift off to sleep, lights are flicked on in my room blinding me, and I am yanked out of bed by Feller and dragged by the arm to the Headmistress's office.

Tilly is standing outside the door, grinning like she just robbed a bank. She stares right at me as I pass and my fist balls up. Feller flings me into the room and the door slams behind me.

Headmistress sits behind her desk and I feel nothing more than terror. She stacks the papers that she was staring at and sets them to the side, and then fingers the gold monocle she was staring through off and her eyes rise to my face. "I understand from Tilly that you've been sneaking around here and going to forbidden areas in the house."

Damn it. What did she see?

Headmistress continues. "You are incorrigible. You blatantly ignore the rules and sometimes I wonder if you are going out of your way to incite trouble. You will go to solitary and you will stay there until I can figure out what to do with you. Get out."

When I slip out of the Headmistress's office, Feller and Tilly are both waiting outside the door. I can tell out of the corner of my eye that Feller has a cartoon carved pumpkin smile on her face and cold chills crawl up my back as she grabs my arm.

I don't bother even telling her to let me go because at this point, I have nothing left in me to fight with. I follow her down the hallway, down the stairs, down another hallway, down more stairs, and into the dungeon. She shoves me into the cold dark room, slamming the door behind me and locking it, and I crumble on the floor into the fetal position.

Things I'll Miss

now that I'm stuck in solitary:

-the ball

-the opportunity to search the property

-pretty much everything that keeps me sane

I Can't Even

tell Kit
or do literally anything about this.

I just have to sit here
twiddling my thumbs.

An even worse thought is
did I manage to screw up
getting out of here?

Surely
more infractions
wouldn't be enough
to disrupt me leaving?

Right?

It's not like I tried to
hurt somebody.

Though I do want to strangle Tilly right now.

Traitor.

But Then My Thoughts Turn

back and I'm stuck on what Kit said again.

I am so mad at him
for saying it, all of it
but I can't help but wonder
if there was at least
some truth to what he said.

Maybe I am in denial.
I spend more time avoiding thinking
about that night than actually
trying to understand what Pierce said
and maybe, more importantly
what he meant.

Maybe me not accepting
"never" as finality
and reminding myself
of the other words too is stupid.

Never
is a big word to work into
I don't know what I want
and Pierce is smart.

He must have thought it through
and had good reasons for saying it.

Perhaps it was my shock
and that it was all just a lot
to go from thinking
we would be in Michigan in 24 hours
to being dumped with a "never"
and a "maybe down the road"
at the same time.

Perhaps that conflicting story
in and of itself
stunts the understanding
I need to gain
keeps me stuck in a soundtrack
looping around and around
and around.

And I guess
if I'm being honest with myself
I haven't really been interested
in gaining an understanding.

All I have wanted is for things
to go back to the way they were.

I wanted to stay
with Pierce in the sweet—
orange peels and tree swings
shared hopes, promised dreams.

But maybe
as painful and as ugly as it is
maybe it is time to face reality.

Maybe
it is time to be eighteen.

And I guess part of being an adult
is figuring out
what do I want for me?

Surprise

A sharp knocking on the door jerks me out of a half awake state, but instead of answering it, I sit and wait. I'm not sure exactly how much time has passed, but it can't be much, certainly not enough for it to be time for me to go.

Then a key turns the door and Kit is standing there in black pants, a white button down shirt, and a server's vest. "Come on, Cinderella," he says, tossing the bag at me. "We've got a ball to go to."

"How in the world…" I stare at him in disbelief. "Also, I don't have a mask. And where's my dress?" I look down. "And I'm filthy."

"You think I didn't think of that?" He pulls two masks out, slips one on covering one eye and holds the other one out to me. Then he steps to the side where I see a large wooden shipping container.

"Okay?" I ask.

"Get in," he says. "I'm going to cart you to my house so you can freshen up really quickly. Your dress is waiting for you there. Dad's away for the weekend, so I've got the house to myself."

Barely believing that this is actually happening, I step into the box. Kit covers me with the lid and I try not to be sick as I go through a series of thumping, bumping, and jolting for what feels like years, although it must just be a few minutes.

Finally the motion stops and light blinds me. I am sitting in the middle of a living room, a couple of old recliners, a loveseat, a TV screen, and brown curtains that match the carpet.

"Bathroom's there," Kit says, gesturing as I climb out of the box. "There's a fresh towel, soap, whatever you need. Dad's girlfriend's door is the one on the right. Probably has some woman type stuff in it. Help yourself. I'm going to change."

I can't remember the last time I got to shower. The second the hot water hits my skin, I feel like a new person. A tropical smelling bar of soap brings refreshment and I want to spend the night under the water. But I'm also excited to get to the ball. I am still wondering if this is a dream, but it feels pretty real, so I'm starting to accept that maybe Kit really is just smart enough to figure this all out.

Wrapping myself in the towel, I slide the "woman stuff" drawer open and find a curling iron and some basic cosmetics, enough for me to pull off a mini transformation.

I barely recognize the person looking back in the mirror at me by the time I am finished. She looks pretty. She looks happy. Who is she? I do a little jig, because for the first time in a long time, I actually feel like a girl again. I haven't felt like this since the morning of graduation.

"I've got your earrings too," Kit says, at the door of the bathroom. I slide my hand out, although I am dressed and still fumbling with the zipper. He did come prepared, I'll give him that, but I'm not about to fluff his ego.

A moment later, I crack the door open and twirl my way into the living room, where Kit is waiting. He holds out his hand and I remind him that I didn't ask for his opinion. "Actually, I was just going to tell you, you look really pretty, Em. That's all."

"What, you think I'm Tilly, in need of your smarmy flattery and attention?"

"In need of it? No. Deserving of it, yes. And it's only fake if I don't mean it, but I do mean it. You really are very pretty."

I gag a little bit in my mouth. I can't deny that it does feel nice to be noticed, but it's time to move along. "So how are we going to get to this thing?" I ask, grabbing Kit's arm, noticing that he cleans up well too. Looks like I'll have a dance partner after all.

"We're going to enter as guests. Are you ready?"

"Never been more," I say, and just the thrill of it has me primed for the adventure.

The Ball

The entire lawn, all the way up to the front porch, is decorated to perfection, floral arrangements, twinkle lights, tables overflowing with food, guests dressed to the nines. It is so beautiful, it is almost unrecognizable.

"Get me one of those fancy drinks," I say to Kit, pushing him toward the refreshment tables.

"So bossy," he says, but he obeys, giving me a chance to inhale an arrangement of hydrangeas.

I remember my initial impressions of Shepley from years ago, similar to this very moment, but so different from my experience of actually living here for the past couple months. And that journey will be coming to an end soon. Tonight, we'll hopefully find Marguerite, and then in 13 days, I'll be on my way.

Kit is at my side again with a flute of champagne in each hand. "You know," he says. "We're not supposed to drink this."

"I thought I wasn't 'supposed to' be hung up on 'supposed to'," I say, taking a sip.

"Pretty sure you don't do anything you're supposed to," he says and laughs. "So you still mad at me, or are we solving a mystery tonight?"

"You give yourself too much credit," I counter. "In order for you to be able to 'make me mad', I'd have to actually listen to what you have to say. Know what I do when your mouth moves? I get up and walk out of here. In my head, I'm gone. Poof. B-bye. Off planet Earth. Away from you."

"Oooh, I'm flattered," he says, falling in line. "My comments take up so much space in your head that you can't even stay on the same planet as me." He flicks at his shoulders and puffs his chest out. "I'm *annoying*."

"You're a turd," I say. "But also, what's a ball without a dance?" I down the rest of my drink and hold my hand out. "Dance with me."

He grins at me. "I thought you'd never ask," and as much as I want to smack him upside the head, I opt for rolling my eyes and copping: "Don't flatter yourself, cowboy."

He takes my glass, sets it beside his on the table, and then takes my hand and pulls me close.

Pierce & I

never danced the night of graduation.

We didn't get a chance to.

Even if he hadn't dumped me
we probably wouldn't have done much dancing
because I was in too much of a hurry
to get on the road.

The course of my life changed
in a matter of hours.

How was I supposed to know
when we romped that morning
before graduation
that it would be the last time
I'd feel his arms wrapped
so tightly around me?

And even now in a moment
where I should be on a dance floor
I'm somewhere else because my future
is right before me and I don't know
what I'm going to do.

Crawling back
and demanding an explanation
is not an option.

The last thing I want is to hear *never* again.

Without the future I thought had my name
written all over it, what is it I want?

Back to Mama?

No, I'm ready to move on
spread my wings.

But if not Mama and if not Pierce
where is my heart calling me?

Less than two weeks
and I will be out of here
the only question left to answer is where?

And out of nowhere
a single solitary idea comes to mind.

Maybe
somewhere
with Annie.

Back to Work

"Good thing I don't get butthurt easily," Kit says, bringing me back to the present. "You are never really here, are you?"

Ignoring his question, I pull out of his arms, walk to one of the refreshment tables, and grab a couple of croissants. Buttery and flaky. Other than the ice cream I had the other day, it has been so long since I've eaten anything that actually tastes good.

"Okay, I'm done," I tell Kit. "Let's do this."

"Really?" he says, as we walk back toward the house. "That's it? You went through all of that, risked so much, just to dance through one song, have a drink, eat a snack, and now you're done?"

"It's just the experience," I say. "You wouldn't understand. Besides, I have a sister to free."

We meet at the top of the tunnel after changing into normal clothes. Armed with flashlights, a metal detector, shovels, and Kit's phone, we sneak out the backdoor, making a run for the solitary garden. The sheer thrill of sneaking back here has my heart racing. I feel alive.

To our great dismay however, we find that the entire garden is filled with flowers matching the one in the envelope, magnificently designed albeit, but a pain for our search nonetheless.

Black dahlias, cosmos, raven's wing, hollyhocks, asters, echinacea, phlox, foxglove. But center to it all, in the back against the shrub wall is a gazebo, one I remember from the portrait set.

"Are you kidding?" Kit says. "I don't think she'd be able to disrupt all of this design. We gotta keep looking."

I shake my head. "There was a portrait of Marguerite and Feller in that gazebo."

Flowers circle it, and as I get closer to the side of the steps, I spot a patch of black lilies. "I think we've found our spot," Kit says, pulling out the metal detector.

Evidence

The party is still raging and it feels like it must be the middle of the night, but we start digging. Just under the edge of the gazebo next to the stairs where the flowers end.

Kit finds pieces of a trash bag first and tearings of a dress, and I find something that clinks when the shovel hits it. I dry heave and Kit steadies me.

"We can stop," he says. "Let's let the authorities do the rest."

I rip out of his hand. "I'm fine. I'm not a baby."

"Never said you were, but it might be gory. Have you ever seen bones before?"

I glare at him. "Have you?"

I crawl out from under the gazebo, and after dry heaving again for a second, say: "Alright, take me back. I'm ready for bed. I'm tired, and I don't want to see anymore that I've already seen."

Kit laughs but I say: "I don't want to hear it. You don't have to sleep in solitary. There's no sleep to be had in there."

He crawls out from the edge and stands up, brushing himself off. "So then what? I go to law enforcement with the evidence and make a report?"

"No," I say. "You have to wait for me. I need to use the information as a bargaining chip with Headmistress so that she'll free my sister."

Kit furrows his brow. "That's a terrible idea, Emily. You have no guarantees and what if Feller comes after you? Besides, you don't even know how long you're going to be in solitary. We can't take that risk."

"Well if the cops come out here and make the arrest, Headmistress might never let them go."

"She might not anyway," Kit says. "That's too much of a risk. You do realize there's still a killer walking around here. She's done it once and I guarantee, she's not going to be too fond of her dirty little secret getting out."

"I need my sister free," I say. "It's only a few more days til my birthday. It can wait that long. Then I'll pack my bag, and after I convince Headmistress, we'll give up the location, head to town, make the report and hopefully, I'll leave from there, if you aren't so Mr. Righteous this time."

Kit isn't sold on the idea, but he helps me rebury the evidence and set things back to the way they were.

Thinking

I make my way back into the dark cell, parting ways with the trash bag I returned my dress to and saying goodnight to Kit. As soon as the door closes and locks behind him, a sinking feeling punches me in the gut.

I'm stuck in here, relying on other people, and absolutely no part of this is within my control at this time. I force myself to think about something else for a moment.

Annie. She must have had a plan. Where was she going to go after leaving here? Something no one seems to know. I feel a roadblock in planning the next part of my life after Shepley, after here, until I know.

Time slows to a halt as I listen to bats, rodents, and who knows what else crawling and flying around. A matter of days until I am out of here. A matter of days until I see my sister. My sister, who, for most of my life, has been a stranger.

If I dig back far enough I can pull a handful of happy memories of us playing together. A few vague and dusty recollections at the bottom of an endless pile of mental illness, rage, and me wishing she would just go away. Feeling relieved when she did.

And now, since being at Shepley in the months that have passed, a brand new pile of feelings has started to grow next to the old. Feelings I have never felt for or about her before.

Curiosity   for the person everyone else sees

Compassion   for everything she went through

Awe   that things weren't worse in our home

Wonder   about where she was planning to go
                and what she was planning to do
                and last but not least

Hope   for a future, where the messy, painful
                relationship we have always had has a
                chance to be set aside
                and we can start something

New

                together

Monotony

Nothing breaks the silence for what seems like a very long time.   I lose track of it, figuring my birthday must be approaching, at which point they have to let me out of here at least for a bit. That is what I'm thinking, I realize, because I don't actually know what they do or don't "have to" do.

The only human interactions I get are meals being chunked through the window three times a day, and depending on who it is, it doesn't necessarily feel human.

If it's something soupy and Tilly is the one delivering, she makes it a point to dump it, so I am left to either do without or scrape it off the ground with my fingers.

So when Kit is the one to bring me a meal today, I almost cry from relief at seeing a friendly face. Even better when he unlocks the door and actually hands me my food instead of throwing it at me.

It doesn't look like food from the gallery either, but a chunk of meat with some mashed potatoes and steamed broccoli.

I'm so happy to see him that I throw my arms around him and absorb the comfort from being close.

"Well, that's the most affection I've gotten from you ever, and that includes when we danced," he says.

I step back. "How did you pull off getting the keys? I can't believe they let you."

"Simple," he shrugs. "I offered to Tilly to bring you food so that she wouldn't have to, and she said okay."

I look at him. "You totally schmoozed her so you could come see me, didn't you?"

He throws his hands up. "It's Tilly, Em. It doesn't take much to get her to cave. Besides, so what if I did? It's not like I like her. I'd think you would like that I found a way to you."

Kit has a point and it does mean something that he came down here to see me, but I don't want his efforts going to his head. "You're gross, but it plays in my favor, so I guess I can't complain."

I take the plate of food and take a huge bite of the meat, oozing flavor. "What's the word?"

"On?" he asks.

"Anything?" I say.

"Well you told me not to say anything, and whether that's the right thing or not, I agreed to it, so we're still waiting on you to get out of here I guess. Have you figured out what you're gonna say to Headmistress?"

"I'm going with a I'll see how it is when I get there approach," I say.

He laughs. "You know, I shouldn't even be surprised. You live your whole life that way, don't you?"

My turn to shrug.

He eyes me. "You're wasting away down here."

"Duh," I say, and I have noticed that my clothes have more and more give each day. "There's no sunlight, the food is terrible, and I haven't had a shower in as many days as I've been down here."

Kit wrinkles his nose. "I was wondering what the smell was."

"Takes one to know one."

He laughs, and then says: "Well, I think they're going to let you out of here soon. The place is falling to shambles upstairs without you."

"I guess I am good for something," I say. "Something other than the obvious, you know, getting in trouble and breaking every rule."

"I should go," he says, holding an arm out.

I glare at him and he says: "Oh, come on. You were so desperate for a hug less than five minutes ago that *you* hugged *me*."

"That was before I smelled you," I say. Truth is, I do want to hug him, but I'm not about to give him the satisfaction, so I pick up the plate of food and start eating while he closes the door.

"Thanks for the food," I shout as an afterthought.

The Beginning of the End

At some unnameable time that I'm guessing is night, a key turns in the door. I have had a few more meals since Kit's visit, so I figure it must be time for me to go.

But there is no one standing there when the door creaks open. I'm creeped out, but not enough to hang out and I wait, so I turn to scan the room quickly before spinning to face the door to make a break for it.

"Not so fast," someone says, and as I come face to face with a crowbar.

Reveal

When I come back to consciousness, it takes me a moment to register where I am and what is happening. My head is pounding and I can barely see in the dimly lit room, but I must still be in the basement, given the building supplies, random tools, and scraps of things scattered around. I also recognize a smell that I have unwillingly grown accustomed to. Bat shit.

I look around. No one is going to hear me down here, if I can even figure out how to get the gag out of my mouth. My hands and feet are tied with thick rope, slashing the skin off my ankles and wrists. I bite into the gag, attempting to tear it with my teeth, but the cloth is too slippery to make any traction.

I can hear someone moving things around on the other side of a pony wall, but I cannot place who. Tilly? No way she would be smart enough, and would she even care to do this to me? No motive.

Headmistress doesn't seem likely either. She could just turn me to stone if she wanted to. Why would she need to go through these motions? Unless this is how she does it.

So maybe it's Headmistress. And if it's not Headmistress, that only leaves one other candidate.

I don't need to wonder for long, as I'm trying to work my wrists together behind my back, but not having much success, because Feller stands up from behind the pony wall, and sidles over to me. "Thought you were going to run with my secret, huh? Thought you were going to save the day let me go to jail? Over my dead body."

I want to get the gag out of my mouth so I can tell her to screw herself. But apparently, I don't need to talk or respond at all for her to think this is her therapy session.

And once she starts spilling, she doesn't stop.

Confession

"You know it's funny," Feller starts with, pacing the room. "I was just saying to myself. I was saying *man, this is the first time in years that she hasn't been totally lost.* I was saying *wow, maybe time truly is finally healing the wound.*

"And then you know what she says to me, right there, in the middle of the party? She says to me, she says: 'Doesn't Emily remind you so much of Annie?' My first thought was—well, no, because well, you're so different from her, so much more of an issue than she ever was, and then my thought was I have a feeling, and I don't know what it was.

"Maybe that you've broken every single rule you could here. I don't know, but something told me I should check. And here we are, you thinking you're being sneaky. You think you've figured me out, huh? You don't know anything. I'm not what you think. I'm not the monster you think I am."

She seems to take the first breath that she has the entire time she has been talking, even refraining from pacing for a moment, just a moment, before she continues on.

"The sadness, Headmistress, it was awful. I couldn't stop her from freezing people. All I could do was cover for her. Help her roll them out to the garden, make up some stories about where they got discharged to. Because keeping them here stopped her. Keeping them here, kept her from crying. I hate to hear her cry.

"My mother left me on the night of a ball. She was supposed to come here to visit me and she never showed. It's the worst day every year since. Every year when Marguerite got her dress, I just wanted that to be me. I wanted to be the one whose mother cared enough to buy me a dress. I couldn't wipe that away, no matter how long I stayed. She had something I would never have.

"That night she showed me her dress like she does every year. It's always terrible. But this time, this time it just—it felt so personal, like she was after me, to remind me of that. I wasn't thinking. All I could see was my mother, and I couldn't stop. I couldn't stop, and there was so much blood on me, on her, on the ground, and when I was done, so was she. I didn't mean to. I didn't set out to. I just lost it, and I lost myself in it."

She's still now and silent, leaning against a support beam pensively. I don't know how much time I have, but I know this is where I'm supposed to stall her. Except that is going to be difficult, given that I can't have a conversation with her. Maybe someone will come down for meal time and disrupt this or maybe I can get my hands free or—I don't know, but I have to keep going. I can't give up.

Feller stares off into space, twirling her wiry curly hair around her finger, and I silently pray that someone needs something from down here. I go through the space in my head, scanning with my eyes and memory to think if there is anything sharp I could make my way to, if I have enough time to do that. Maybe she hasn't figured out what to do with me yet and maybe I have time. Maybe she'll have to leave for something and I'll have a chance.

"You're the jealous type, aren't you?" she muses, bringing me back. "Don't think I am judging—I understand jealousy best. But one thing I don't understand, Emily Anne Jones, is why you didn't just stay away? You had all you needed with your mother. But it wasn't enough, was it?

"Playing the wounded sister game, like someone wouldn't remember that Annie never had a sister. You thought you could fool me. You thought I was stupid. You just had to come back here and tell everyone what you found out the first time. You just had to be the hero, didn't you? Well, I'm not going to let that happen."

She disappears behind the pony wall, and I start praying that whatever method she chooses is fast and as painless as possible. If I can't escape, if someone doesn't find me, if there's no way out, I just hope that whatever she has in mind is over quickly.

Rescue

I recognize the footsteps immediately. Kit. Relief oceans over me, but then I realize, if I can hear him, so can Feller, if she is still behind the wall, plotting whatever she is plotting. He needs to be quieter. I urge him in my head to lighten his footsteps, but he's moving with purpose. And then there's a second set of footsteps, but not in time to spare Kit.

Feller has attacked him with something and I hear him fall to the floor, but within seconds of his body hitting the cold cement floor, Headmistress screams at Feller: "You despicable cow!"

Feller is now in my line of sight, trying to escape Headmistress, who is lunging for her. "How dare you? I took you in as my own. I loved you. Marguerite loved you."

"It's not what you think," Feller screams back, dodging and weaving between beams and piles, coming in and out of sight. "It's not what you think, whatever you think. I swear!"

"Cops are on their way," Kit says loudly, coming back to consciousness. "Better stop." He sees me, and I plead with my eyes.

Feller is confused now, looking quickly back and forth between the two of us, giving the Headmistress a chance to grab a hold of her by the hair and rip her to the ground. Here's a fight I never thought I'd witness and never wanted to. It's the most intense cat fight I've ever seen, pulling hair, biting, scratching, but all that comes to me is more relief when Kit cuts the restraints off my hands and feet. I pull the gag out and say: "Jackass."

I'm not sure how to break the fight up without getting pulled into it myself, but I need Headmistress to get out of it, so that I can convince her to set everyone free.

I slip around the corner grabbing the copper pipe that Feller must have hit Kit over the head with. "Can you get her with this?" I say, handing it to Kit. "We have to get Headmistress out to the garden before the cops get here."

Free

Together, we carry Headmistress up the stairs, although it is more like dragging, out to the garden. She is limp in arm and barely weighs anything, her dress clearly disguising how thin she is.

We sit her up in the middle of the garden and Kit runs to get her a cup of water. I sit down beside her, her face expressionless.

"The cops are on their way," I say, like I hadn't already told her that numerous times before. "I need you to let everyone go. Please."

She stares off into the distance, responseless.

"Please," I say. "I know Marguerite was everything. And she's gone. And I know there is nothing I can say that will take that pain from you. From any of us. I miss her dreadfully. But the rest of me that I left here when I escaped—she's still here. And you love her too. And you love Nat and Ronnie and all the others. Please set them free. Please don't do to us what was done to you."

I don't even recognize the words coming out of my own mouth. Pleading, honest to God, vulnerable pleading brought out here on behalf of the other part of me. Someone whose name I didn't even mention before coming here. Someone I've grown to love. Someone I want to find within me again.

Headmistress is still leaning against me, and my words don't seem to spark even the slightest reaction, but I need to believe that they can. I need to believe that they will.

When Kit returns with the water, she takes a sip and then falls back against me.

"Please," I say again, and this time, when I do, she slowly flips her wrists so her palms face up and holds them midair. They begin to quiver, but she still holds them, and I think she must be on the verge of a stroke or something. The look on Kit's face is one of shock, horror and awe, and I turn to take in his view.

The statues emerge gradually from stone to flesh, from dead to alive.

Headmistress crumbles to the ground and I see Annie running toward me, and I finally find the part of me that has been missing, as she crashes into me and it all starts coming back to me.

I remember everything that I left here.

Part of Me

Part of me left
part of me disappeared
part of me was lost
part of me I held dear.

Part of me was captured
inside of an experience
Part of me never went home
and it was a part of me I needed.

Part of me was surviving
until I started to remember
another part of me who struggled
with memories she couldn't decenter.

Part of me I welcome back
She kept me alive too
by bringing me to today
shouldering the burden of truth.

Part of me knows I wouldn't be here
I won't demand her silence again
I welcome and cherish every part
Not one will be forgotten.

Mama

Mama didn't end up going to Europe after all and she makes the trip to come and get me even though I tell her she doesn't have to. "I want to, baby. I want to."

When I see her pulling up the driveway, I run to the car and crumble into her arms. "Emily, my girl. I'm so sorry. I had no idea. This whole time. This whole time."

There's something I know—and that's some of this Mama will never know, and by default, will never understand.

But I don't think she has to.

The New Plan

Find my way with Nat
who is just as stubborn and expressive
as Laurel had said
and start something new
in the gulf of Mississippi.

Nat still wants to go
and we beg Laurel to come with us.

Shepley House
is being put up
for sale

all of its patients
sent to different homes
so it's not like Laurel
can stay.

But Laurel doesn't feel safe
in the outside world.

Says it is too much for her
so we search
for care facilities in Mississippi
so we can visit her.

Goodbye

Kit holds out a perfect box, wrapped in striped paper. "A goodbye gift," he says.

I accept it, eyeing him suspiciously.

"Oh go on and open it," he urges.

I pull the wrapping paper off to reveal a perfect white box. I slip the lid off. Wrapped in tissue paper are a set of paint brushes and a couple of small canvases.

I place the lid back on the box and set it on the bench beside me, and then wrap my arms around him. "Thank you," I say.

He hugs me back, before pulling away and staring at my eyes for a second. "You know, Em, I happen to know of one boy who would have been in that getaway car with you in a heartbeat."

"Yeah, whatever," I say, but I can't help but reach up and run my fingers through Kit's curls. He smiles, leaning into my hand and then leans forward, his hand holding mine in place, and pecks me on the cheek.

"Some other time, some other life," he says, pulling away. "You'd be my girl."

I roll my eyes at him. "I wouldn't go that far."

He laughs, then says: "All that stuff with Pierce and everything, don't worry about it. You never know how it might work out in the end, but you should just focus on figuring yourself out."

"Not that I asked for your opinion," I remind him.

He shrugs. "As long as he takes up that much space in your head, well...it isn't really fair to anyone else, huh?"

"Too much for you?" I laugh.

"Oh, I still think you're gorgeous and I would kiss you a thousand times over, but I think your heart is pretty occupied right now. You'll find Pierce someday or maybe you won't, but either way, you'll be okay. That is one thing I'm totally sure of." He shrugs. "Besides....there's more to life than love."

I lean against him. "It's gonna take me some time, but I'll send you a check eventually."

He laughs. "I won't hold my breath."

Twisted

"What do you mean, you're over him now?" Mama asks. "Over who?"

"You know, my ex. Pierce," I say.

"What?" Mama says, still confused. "Your friend?"

"Oh yeah, duh," I correct myself. "Of course that's what I meant."

Mama nods. "Ah. Yes." She's thoughtful for a moment, then says: "You know, it all came as such a surprise to me, finding out you liked him like that. I had no idea. I don't think anyone knew, not even Pierce himself. You never really let on to be interested in boys or any of that stuff. That's why we were all thrown off when you started going off on him at the party. You guys had always been the best of buds. It didn't make sense that you were flipping out on him for wanting to go to college. It was his forever plan. All he was trying to say, I think, was that he just wanted to stay friends with you, not be more. But I guess you understand that now."

I shrug. "We all get a detail or two twisted sometimes."

Author's Note

Perception is a funny thing.

Acknowledgments

I wrote this story in 2022 and then tabled it for three years, but there was someone who loved it and made me believe in it from the beginning. Danielle Zell, thank you for helping me bring this story to life and for being by my side through all of it. You made me believe I could write this.

Kelly Heard, thank you for believing in me and my voice. I owe so much of the confidence in this story to you.

Thank you Luisa Galstyan for the beautiful cover and for making my vision come to life.

Thank you Haley Reinhart, Michael Buble, Ella Fitzgerald, Postmodern Jukebox, Tony Bennett, Katharine McPhee, Liza Minnelli, ABBA, Marvin Gaye, Kristen Chenoweth, Faith Hill, Lake Street Dive, and Billy Joel for shaping the feel of this story.

To my kids and kitties, thank you for being a steady source of humor, inspiration, and distraction.

To my reader, I am grateful and honored to have you here. It truly means the world to me. Thank you to the moon and back. <333

This book started with a dedication to you and will end the same way. Thank you, Mom, for being my first reader and for believing in me. I didn't dream you'd like this one, and I'm still honestly kind of surprised that you do, but it means the most to me that you're willing to wander into my world with an open mind. Even when it's experimental. I love you.

About

Monica J. Linder is a writer from Roseville, California. She lives in Augusta, Maine with her two kids and a whole bunch of kitties. This is her second novel.